PECKINPAH

An Ultraviolent Romance

by
D. HARLAN WILSON

Illustrated by
DANNY EVARTS

RAW DOG
SCREAMING
PRESS

Peckinpah: An Ultraviolent Romance © 2013 by D. Harlan Wilson
ISBN 978-1-935738-40-4

Second Paperback Edition, September 2013

All rights reserved. Published by Raw Dog Screaming Press in Bowie, MD. Printed in the United States of America. First paperback edition published in 2009 by Shroud Books.

Book Design, Layout & Illustrations © 2009, 2013 by Danny Evarts
www.DannyEvarts.net

Cover art © 2013 by Matthew Revert
www.matthewrevert.com

Introduction © 2012 by Ian Cooper

Edited by Travis Manderbean
www.TheKyotoMan.com

Raw Dog Screaming Press
Bowie, MD

www.RawDogScreaming.com

For my brother David, who showed me the Way of Sam.

ALSO BY D. HARLAN WILSON

TABLE OF CONTENTS

AN INTRODUCTION BY IAN COOPER

It´s there at the beginning of Chapter 30, in black and white: "This is a book about the telling of ultraviolent deeds." You can´t say you weren´t warned. It´s not a book for everyone. But you knew that anyway. The clue is in the title. Sam Peckinpah was the soft-spoken, coke-addled, drunken madman who aestheticized violent death, produced a fistful of rape/ seduction scenes, pissed his name on a cinema screen and gave us a protagonist who starts the day popping his pubic lice.

The initial set-up of D. Harlan Wilson´s book is a familiar one. A bunch of bad guys turn up in a quiet town and wreak bloody havoc. It could be *The Wild One*. Or even better, *The Wild Bunch*, which starts with Pike Bishop and his gnarled and drink-weathered compadres riding into town while kids watch a scorpion and a horde of ants duking it out out as they burn.

But this gets a lot weirder—and maybe even a lot bloodier. Felix Soandso, the closest thing here to a hero, is a wronged man who seeks violent revenge, a David Sumner-esque little guy forced to find his killer within. The bad guys are the Fuming Garcias, a band of snappily dressed psychotics, like a cross between The Ramones (they're not related either) and Alex´s

Droogs. Their leader is the terrifying Samson Thataway (I kept picturing Al Lettieri at his most brutish, wearing Nick Cave's hair).

Presiding over all of it, impassive behind mirror-shades, is Saint Sam, the patron saint of violence, disillusion and chaos. There are many direct references here: a concise biography, a description of the Monty Python sketch "Sam Peckinpah's Salad Days," mentions of *The Rifleman* and *The Osterman Weekend*, Borgnine and Coburn, a Julian Lennon song, an actress terrorized by a filmmaker, an Alias and a dead Gila monster. But there are plenty of other strange refracted images and situations that may well be Peckinpavian if you think about them long enough: the pregnant girl in the white dress, Tennessee Williams, Felix Soandso's locket which contains his own picture, a man who commits a crime and then sets out to solve it. When Felix steps out of his house only to get a clod of wormy earth thrown in his face, it is reminiscent of the weird scene in *Pat Garrett and Billy the Kid* (cut from the original release) where Garrett gets drawn into a shooting match with a stranger floating down river on a raft. It's a hostile world, both these scenes seem to say, one where a bullet or a faceful of worms can just come out of nowhere at any time and fuck you up.

But the director is more than a motif here. His uncompromising, contradictory persona and his even more uncompromising films permeate the book—subject and theme, style and (in every sense of the word) execution. Before the cocaine and the booze got too much for even the battle-hardened Sam to cope with, his working method was unique (and to producers and studio backers, uniquely maddening). There was no Hitchcock-style "editing in the camera" but rather a lot of cameras shooting a lot of film—often at a lot of different speeds—which would then be painstakingly cut together in a bewildering montage, elliptical, fragmented and jagged. The prose here has a similar disorientating effect, a frenzy of images and sounds, a broken, scrambled structure and a tone which shifts on a dime-sized blood spot from the sweet and tender to the dizzyingly wild and brutal, the hysterically funny to the hideous. It is, to borrow Wilson´s description of a pulp sci-fi paperback, "as comical as it is serious."

Peckinpah used genre all the time but not in the way that, say, Hitchcock or John Ford did. He was interested in stretching it and stripping it down, mixing and matching, bending, folding, spindling and mutilating it. So *Bring Me the Head of Alfredo Garcia* is western and horror film, romance and thriller, love story and autobiography, blackly comic parody and buddy movie about a guy and a rotting head.

The book you are holding in your hands takes this idea of generic chaos and ramps it up, presenting a very funny and extremely violent mix of more genres, sub-genres, styles and cycles than you can shake a very sharp, bloody stick at. (See if you can spot the *Friday the 13th* reference). Reviewers keep falling back on calling it a science fiction story, presumably as it´s the only genre in which you can do pretty much anything you want. Anyone who knows a bit about Peckinpah, especially his hatred for all things new, from cars to children—he once opined that "the problem started when they discovered the wheel"—might find it heretical to invoke his name in relation to sci-fi. But he was one of the writers of the paranoid classic

Invasion of the Bodysnatchers (look quickly as you can see him playing a meter man!) and one of his many thwarted projects was *Castaway*, a Twilight Zoney post-apocalyptic novel by James Gould Cozzens.

And there´s more here, including a whole bunch of things and hints and asides, some that I didn´t catch but you just might. Soap operas and camera angles, computer cleaner and superglue, that all-pervading pigshit smell and a very jaundiced, truly terrifying view of Middle Amerika, all chain stores and tanning booths, fast food and violent death, a kind of Hieronymus Bosch goes to Indiana.

In 1972, Peckinpah gave an interview to William Murray, at the end of which he said: "Sometimes I want to say the hell with it and pack it in but I can´t do that. I stick or I know I´m nothing. Then I look around and I notice I´m not entirely alone. There are maybe seventeen of us left in the world. And we´re a family. That family is composed of the cats who want to do their number and get it on." After reading this book, Sam, I think you can stretch it to eighteen . . .

Neuss, December 2012

Ian Cooper is a screenwriter, editor, and author of a cultography on *Bring Me the Head of Alfredo Garcia* published by Columbia University Press.

The basic male act, by its very nature, starts out as an act of physical aggression, no matter how much love it eventually expresses.

I find color and vitality and meaning in the loser. The outcast is the individualist. I'm not concerned with Everyman. I see color, conflict, a wish for something better, in the man who strikes out for himself. I'm talking about people who are not sheep.

I'm a whore. I go where I'm kicked. But I'm a very good whore.

—S.P.

PECKINPAH

An
Ultraviolent
Romance

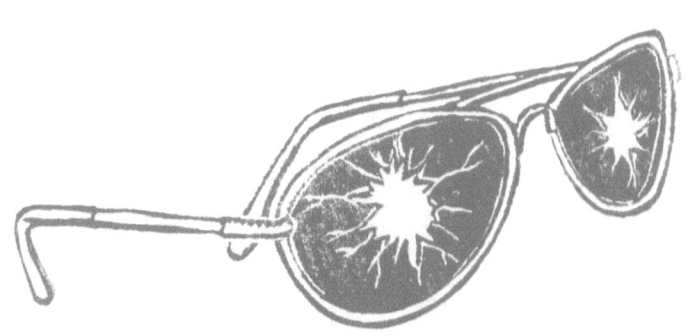

Entr'acte

Revenge tragedy. Exploding wounds. The birth of everyday life.

Peckinpah.

2

The Stranger

This is what happens: a stranger drives a long blue car into a small Midwestern town and murders all of its registered voters. He quickly forgets about the murders, though, and tries to solve them. He fails. He diagnoses himself with a run-of-the-mill multiple personality disorder and blames the crime on one of his alter-egos. He arrests himself, processes himself, incarcerates himself. In jail, he writes a letter of apology to the mayor of the small Midwestern town promising him that voting booths can't whistle in the wind forever. Then he writes a suicide note.

Dear Stranger, begins the note . . .

But he can't do it.

He breaks out of prison and walks towards the silos.

Mise en Scéne

Skid marks all over the faded green exterior of the Casey Jones fryhouse. A guilty-looking ATV near the dumpster. Pickup trucks and Buicks and motorcycles in the parking lot. Gravel. Cement blocks. Pigshit. Distant rattle of train tracks. A dimly lit sign; last week Tuesday's special; letters missing from each word. Black grease and burnt meat. Telephone poles. A sharp chimney pipe. Slow curls of smoke.

Sky.

4

Odeur en Scène

Pigshit.

Fertilization of the Gods

A big, garish church situated across from a small, unassuming church whose brown-green yards have been fertilized with pigshit.

6

The Old Bastard Car Wash

Just when the critical sun had passed, they walked into the water, and the lights flashed blue and red, blue and red, blue and red . . . This is the place in which one must follow the rules. Rules are like branches. They can grow, or they can be snapped off and fed into a woodchipper . . .

The streets were always under construction, yet nobody had seen a construction worker for years. They abandoned their bright yellow vehicles on sidewalks and yards and boardwalks. But sometimes the vehicles moved. And sometimes work got done . . .

At the Old Bastard Car Wash, a retiree in a trucker hat tended to a customer. The customer drove up to the gate, rolled down his window and inserted a credit card into the machine.

Processing . . . processing . . . processing . . .

The retiree leapt off of his perch and scampered over to the customer. "Put yer card in," he said.

"Pardon me?"

"Put yer card in. Put it in. Like this." He made a stiff inserting motion.

"I put it in already."

"No. Do it like this now." He made another, slower inserting motion.

"Ok."

"No. Like this."

"I put it in already."

"You see how I'm doing it now?"

"Yes. Thank you."

"This is my job, boy. Don't thank me."

"Ok."

"Ok my granny's asshole." The retiree's tongue wagged and salivated as he showed the customer how to pay for the car wash with increasing urgency.

The customer said, "It's processing. Look. It's processing." He pointed at an LED screen.

"Jesus help me!" The retiree's prosthetic leg fell off. He collapsed. He retrieved the leg and struggled to put it back on. "Don't fergit now!" he grunted. "Don't fergit to put yer card in there you dumb motherfucker!"

The customer pulled into the car wash. An aluminum door closed behind him. Across the street, the colorful lights of a Sonic Drive-In entranced hungry farmers and factory workers . . .

Warlock Heroes

The smell of pigshit coincided with multiple slippages on dogshit. The slippages all occurred as residents walked into the respective front doors of their employers. Some of the residents caught themselves before falling down. Some fell down. One broke bones.

Three weeks later, this headline in the newspaper:

Woman slips on expletive, gets broke

And eviscerated from the subsequent article, this string of words: ". . . acute correlation with Harry Potterlike devilry. One doesn't make heroes out of warlocks. One tortures and kills warlocks with a child's inquisitive abandon . . ."

8

Dollars & Common Cents

Every store was a Dollar Store or a Dollar General or a Family Dollar that charged more than a dollar for each piece of merchandise. Town Hall throbbed and snorted like a congenital heart. Breakfast (incl. three whole eggs, two strips of bacon, one slice of white toast and a snotpile of grits) cost $6.99 at The Chowbaby Eathouse. *The Osterman Weekend* was the feature presentation at the Nameless One Screen Movie Theater. Obese insects exploded onto windshields. Fire engines died and had to be towed to the burning buildings. Tsunami of church hymns. Shitscape of cornfields. A train went by; the ventriloquist doll in the caboose gave onlookers the finger. Throats. High school football players. Common cents.

Burger-king-mcdonalds-taco-bell-wendys-arbys-walmart-dairy-queen-hot-dog-stand-red-lobster-shitty-italian-bistro.

Clouds hung overhead like mastitic udders.

Cold Beers at the Lake

At roughly 13,500 square feet, it was the biggest inland lake in Indiana. At a shallow depth of five to seven feet, it was the dirtiest inland lake in the Amerikan Midwest. They built it in the nineteenth century as a reservoir for the Miami and Erie canals. At the turn of the century, they discovered oil in the surrounding area and installed a series of derricks in the water. Farmland encircled 90 percent of the lake, drooling runoff day and night. On clear days the lake adopted a lizard green hue; on cloudy days it turned steel gray.

The lake housed innumerable catfish that died in apocalyptic numbers on a daily basis, bloated corpses gurgling to the surface. Distressed, the lake's resolute fisherman quickly harvested and reanimated the corpses with jumper cables attached to lawn mowers. When the fish came back to life, they either returned them to the water or placed them on asphalt and smashed their brains to shit with sledgehammers. Then they assiduously cracked open cold beers . . .

A stranger rented a pontoon boat and took it out to the middle of the lake. He kneeled down and dipped his finger into the water. He counted to twenty. The thing he removed resembled a decayed chili pepper. He put a bandage on it and looked around . . . People waterskied. People swam and bathed and had mud fights. People filled glasses with lakewater and drank it like lemonade . . .

Now and then a group of semi-ecoconscious plumbers got sober enough to act on their *Grün* hopes and desires. They strategically converged on different parts of the lake with ten-foot plungers, pumping out muck and sewage and toxins and shit and bones and viscera and oil and furniture and Vorheeses and sludge in geyseral bursts. Such good-willed blitzkriegs usually didn't last that long, however, as the plumbers always brought plenty of cold beers with them.

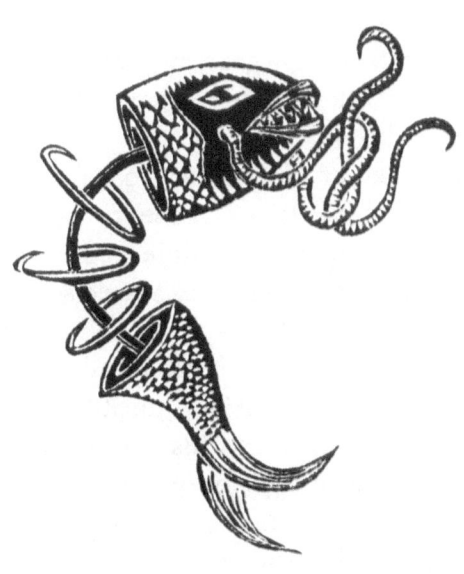

10

They Reinstated Public Executions

The bank robber tried to escape on a goat.

The police followed him for miles in jacked up Mustangs, all the way to Blue Lick, waiting for the goat to tire out. It didn't.

They pulled over the bank robber. "Can I help you, officers?" he said.

"Step off the escape goat, sir," said the officers, and arrested him. A legend grew. They called it "The Great Goat Chase."

In the wake of "The Great Goat Chase," they reinstated public executions . . . The criminal was ordered to lie down on a scaffold. An executioner wearing overalls and a blowtorch mask placed a sheet of wood atop him. Then, one at a time, an orchestra of fat women stepped onto the wood—sound of a harsh, increasingly metallic shriek—until the criminal lost his breath and died and his sap drained into the gutters. They filled the empty cadaver with straw for use as a scarecrow. A merry public event. As residents took turns stuffing the body, one handful at a time, with transubstantiational relish, they set up arts and crafts stations over there, and a Salisbury steak sandwich stand over there, and right over there Danny Fingerhut's band Danny Fingerhut & the Hotrod Icicles set up their equipment . . .

There were no crows in Dreamfield.

They Grew Chainsaws in the Cornfields

They grew chainsaws in the cornfields . . . Image of freckled teenage redheads shucking ears and revealing the weapons at the core. One weapon after another, hand over fist. They tossed them into wheelbarrows and, at the end of the day, rolled them to the grocery store for processing . . . processing . . . processing . . .

Chainsaw soup. Chainsaw stroganoff. Chainsaw à la carte. Chainsaw spongecake. And a stochastic appetite for destruction . . .

Sometimes the corn grew improperly. Instead of chainsaws, the husks revealed anthropomorphous heads. Usually the heads were autistic, but sometimes they could speak clearly, of their own volition, with a minimum of echolalia, and on occasion they turned out to be dynamic conversationalists and debaters, until their interlocutors got bored and plucked and boiled them.

Sometimes a shucked ear rendered nothing but hot black tar.

. . . He let the tar flow onto his hand. It burned. His mouth opened into a frozen scream. The tar singed his skin as it trickled down his wrist and forearm. He squeezed the ear harder. Black tongues leapt at his face like sewer rats . . . His hand began to melt. His lips trembled . . . Silence. Bright purple blood mixed with the tar and flesh dripped onto the toe of his shoe like candle wax. Soon the weathered tips of the ulna and the radius made an appearance. They glowed whiter and whiter as the tar progressed down his forearm to his unsuspecting elbow . . . Starblazer eyes. Transcendentalist horror. The incomprehensibility of death.

Nothing.

The tar cooled. Hardened.

His mouth closed like a book. He used cornhusks to bandage the nub.

. . . "I'm home!" he announced, striding into the kitchen. He stopped smiling when he saw her. He held up his arm. "My hand committed suicide."

"Hands do things," she said, preoccupied by a pile of ground beef she didn't seem to know what to do with. Arms akimbo, she stared at the beef as if it had told her a lie.

"Didn't you hear me? I said my hand is dead. Not only that—it's gone. An ear of corn ate it. I'm free!"

"What am I going to do with this old meat? I don't know what to do with it."

"I don't care what you do with it long as you cook it good. I'm hungry. I've had a busy day."

She looked askance at him. "How will you eat without your hand?"

"I have another hand." He showed her.

"I've never seen you eat with that hand before. Do you know how?"

He looked at the hand. "I don't know." He laughed. "How hard can it be?"

Following his lead, she laughed, too. They went on and on and then abruptly fell silent.

. . . He sat at the table, pensive, distressed, hovering over a carefully crafted 16 oz. patty centered on a plastic plate. To the left of the plate rested a hand, fingertips pressed firmly into the dinner table, except for the index finger, which gesticulated wildly, as if possessed . . .

Drive-In Movie Theater

Sky the color of uncooked fowl. Dead signage with no visible titles. Abandoned. Expansive gravel pit. Tread marks from Herculean pickup trucks. Tumbleweed. Skeletal trees, skeletal bushes. Telephone poles. Dead smokestacks on the outskirts. Cinderblock outhouse and concession stand in the middle of the pit, haunted by the ghosts of hotdogs, caramel corn, candy bars, Slurpees, eight lb. bowel movements . . . The movie screen looms over the pit. A sad and dispossessed employee.

Hog Ripping

"I can rip just about anything in half." Billy Seersucker started with a sheet of vellum followed quickly by a slice of cheese. Neither feat garnered much acclaim, so he moved on to a quarter, a picnic basket, and finally a hardcover edition of *War and Peace*.

Spectators observed him with bovine expectancy.

"What about this here hog?"

The farmer pushed his way to the front of the crowd. He removed a choke-chain from the hog's neck and kicked it in the shin. He kicked it again. The hog crept forward, glancing nervously over its shoulders. It emitted a subdued oink.

Billy Seersucker knelt and clicked his tongue. The hog came closer. He reached out his hand. It sniffed and licked his fingers.

He stood and circled the hog, gauging its distribution of poundage. Most of the weight appeared to be in its haunches, although its oversized head gave Seersucker second thoughts, and its pot-belly commanded his attention, too. He looked into the hog's eyes. It oinked at him assertively.

He lifted the hog over his head and ripped it in half.

Offal exploded across the sky like the pulp of screaming watermelons . . .

"My hog!" shouted the farmer, falling on the carcass. He struggled like a child to stuff the swine's entrails back into its severed halves. "I loved this damned hog! It was a prize hog! God help me!"

The crowd became unruly, but their tempers weren't beyond repair. Things didn't really start to get out of hand until a slot technician dared Billy Seersucker to rip his vending machine in half . . .

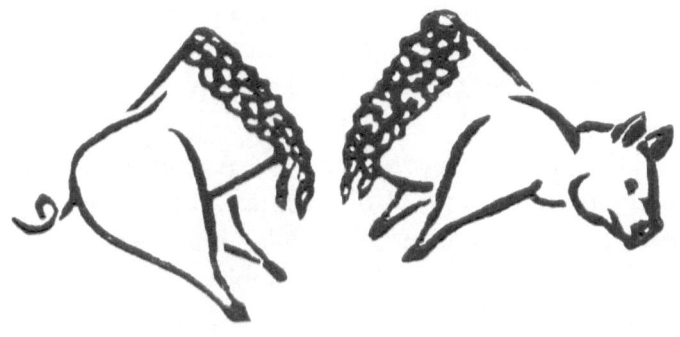

14

Walk-a-lator, Etc.

The walk-a-lator divided the desert into equal halves. They put on grey suits and red ties and rode it all the way to the perimeter. Camels galloped everywhere. Planes crashed everywhere.

Cacti. Dust devils. Horses and more camels and souped-up Gila monsters . . .

This is what happened next: A Wal-Mart shopper tripped in the frozen pizza aisle. Her skirt flapped over her head and exposed a mad hatter. "My goodness!" she shouted. Concerned frowns rivaled expressions of mortal surprise. Later, outside in the parking lot, the same thing happened, only this time she fell into a crack in the hippopotamus night . . .

"Ararrrrrgle!" (Trans. "Thanks for shopping at Wal-Mart!")

Later, back inside Wal-Mart . . . A pharmacist sexually assaulted one of his techies. She fought him off with a tranquilizer gun, nailed him with at least six darts, but he was a big sonofabitch, and he was a sexcrazed sonofabitch, and eventually the sonofabitch overpowered her. At first she screamed. Then she moaned. Then she sighed. When it was over, the pharmacist pulled up his brown pants and buttoned up his white jacket and he and the techie calmly raided the refrigerator of its surplus benzodiazapine and norepinephrine reuptake inhibitors.

"Ararrrrrgle!" (Trans. "Thanks again for shopping at Wal-Mart!")

. . . speeding down the interstate in an unassuming 4-door sedan. A cop pulls the sedan over and says to the driver: "Good morning, sir. Do you know how fast you were going?"

"Yes," said the driver. "I have an odometer in this automobile. It tells me."

Nodding, the cop spit tobacco juice over his shoulder, then placed the cold barrel of a standard issue sidearm into his mouth.

He fired. He fired. He fired. He fired.

Four buckets of brains splashed across the lost highway in the brown dawn . . .

Felix Soandso awoke. Abjected, he sat up in bed. The bed moved smoothly across a walk-a-lator in the desert. He was alone.

Gust of swinefunk.

He passed a team of blacksmiths trying to solder wings onto a tank. They were fibrous and looked real. Pterodactyl wings.

He passed a team of surgeons in OR uniforms and gas masks crucifying a flatscreen television. They nailed the corners of the television into the cross with long relics. Together they erected the cross like soldiers erecting the Amerikan flag at Iwo Jima. Playing on the television was a rendition of Tennessee Willliams' *The Glass Menagerie*. The actors cried out and coughed blood when the surgeons pounded in the relics, then diplomatically returned to their business.

He passed a herd of ape-men dancing and morphing back and forth between ape-men and talk show hosts.

He passed a thin male waiter with a thin black mustache brandishing a martini on a silver platter. The waiter glared at him like an uninvited guest . . .

The walk-a-lator went on and on and on and on and then somebody unplugged it.

Felix Soandso got out of bed and wrangled a camel. He climbed between the humps. They fell into a stiff trot. They accelerated into a breakneck gallop.

They glided across the desert towards a distant forest, dodging plane crashes, leaping over fiery debris and screaming carcasses . . .

First Theory of Ultraviolence

A pregnant girl in a white dress. Brick walls. When a full moon emerges in the afternoon sky. When drivers don't think about putting on turn signals. Soft fiesta music. A tobacco shop. Snack food. The resolute sociopathology of little round men and their gendered subordinates. 40 ft. containers of horny goat weed. Incomprehensibly gigantic solar flares. An alien race of inflatable appliances rapping on the back door of the universe. Cut back to Dreamfield— to a paradigmatic mind's screen . . . Bullets tore into flesh. Hombres transformed into soft machines riddled with lipstick gashes that wheezed and cursed and projectile-vomited the blood of roses. Knives relieved jugulars of their corporeal obligations. Batons twirled over the innerspatial panorama of gore as B-movie monstrosities tore down the sky like Yellow Wallpaper . . . Suddenly his eyeball popped out like a champagne cork and a handheld minicam crammed itself through the gaping socket. It couldn't fit. Thus the minicam ate his head, brains first, with zombified gusto, from the inside-out. Then it surrogated his head, fusing wires and fiberoptics with skin and veins and bone.

His body used one arm to tear off the other arm. Rigor mortis set in almost immediately. The body clasped hands with the amputated arm and leaned on it like a cane, forming a relatively stable tripod atop which the minicam shot footage . . . Clink of beer bottles. Fetishism of reality. Ultraviolence as the only solution, the gateway to de-*cog*-nition, the cure for the virus of the Middle Amerikan real . . .

Stillness.

Quiet.

Quiet as an unlit candle.

Quiet as a cathedral on Monday morning.

Quiet as the shell of a cicada on a window screen overlooking a reservoir smooth as glass . . .

. . . The following is a dramatization. It must be taken very seriously.

A clover grew out of a crack in the sidewalk. It lived a long life. Then somebody stepped on it and broke its pale stem.

The clover blew away.

Pseudoexistentialism 101

Narrative precedes existence precedes essence . . .
Pseudoexistentialism 101.

. . . The farmer missed his hog. Blind faith assured
him that he would see the hog again, one day, in heaven.
But what would he do in the meantime? How would he
cope with the grief?

"People don't understand how smart hogs is," he
told his son, Matthew Mark Luke John Cobberly, a
chemistry teacher at Dreamfield Central High School.
"That old hog was a smart old hog. Sometimes when
nobody was looking we'd sit back up in the kitchen up
there and play gin rummy! Hamlet even beat me from
time to time. I even learned him to stand up and walk
around on his hind legs! He could walk real good and
nice. Next week I was gonna learn him how to do the
catwalk! I was gonna learn him that!"

The farmer paused.

Matthew Mark Luke John Cobberly said, "That pause
you just made is pregnant with meaning. I suspect if
the pause continues, it will give birth to entire legions
of significance, connotations and innuendos. And I will
be the one with egg on my face."

The farmer didn't say anything for awhile; he stood there with his mouth half open. Then his lips twitched and he shook his head and said, "Son, goddamn it, that just don't make no sense now. Boy, what is you talking about? Ain't no eggs on nobody's faces, for Chrissake. Nobody's giving birth to nothing. I was just done talking, is all. It wasn't no pause. It was the end."

"The end," sighed Matthew Mark Luke John Cobberly, deflating like a tire.

Felix Soandso Goes to Work

Felix Soandso kept a locket around his neck. Inside was a picture of himself. If somebody knocked him out and he got amnesia, this way he could look at the locket and remember who he was.

Helen put out her cigarette, turned over onto her stomach, and stretched out so that her head rested on the foot of the bed. She could see Felix's reflection in the bathroom mirror as he ran a straight razor up and down his neck. She studied the precision with which he maneuvered the blade. Hardly the way she shaved her legs, a feat she performed haphazardly, almost dangerously, as fast as she could go. She admired Felix's patience and restraint; few men she had ever known performed everyday routines with efficiency. Then again, she used a disposable razor on her legs, not a straight razor, and no matter how fast she shaved, she was never in jeopardy of slicing off a nostril or exhuming a jugular.

"I see you looking at me," said Felix. Not true, techncally; in the mirror he could only see the curve of her ass. But he could usually tell what she was thinking and doing when he looked at her ass, naked or otherwise.

Helen said, "I'm not looking at you."

"I know what you're doing. I can see your ass."

"That's crude."

"Crude, but true." The straight razor didn't waver as he spoke. "I might as well tell you that I suspect your ass of hard knowledge. Or at least fossilized knowledge. Know the difference? There isn't any. But I think your ass has a brain. There's a piece of your brain in your ass, I mean. They're connected. I don't know how it got down there. Obviously it climbed down the ladder of your spine, but how does that happen? Maybe it didn't happen. Maybe a bud of cerebral tissue bloomed on your coccyx, forming a brain-flower. This brain-flower is connected to the brain in your head—let's call this one the brain-fist. The brain-flower is connected to the brain-fist by way of the spine. At the same time, the brain-flower is simultaneously self-sustaining and capable of independent thought, much to the brain-fist's chagrin. The brain-flower doesn't have a mouth and it's too sophisticated, mature and hygienic to appropriate your anus as a speaking instrument. It must therefore communicate telepathically, although not in a verbal context. Not with me, at least. All of the messages your ass sends me are imaginary, which is to say, in the form of images. The message I just received showed me a picture of you staring at me. Hence my remark: 'I see you looking at me.' I wasn't lying."

Felix watched Helen's hand reach back and squeeze a cheek, as if making sure it existed. "I guess that's funny," she said "It might not be so funny, though. It's totally juvenile, right? Ass humor is for little boys."

"Have you ever read *Ulysses*? There's ass humor on every page. Are you calling James Joyce a creep?"

"No. I'm calling him a little boy."

He put down the razor and rinsed off his face with a washcloth. What did Helen see in him? She was too good-looking for him. She was too smart for him. She was too level-headed for him. She was too fashionable and successful for him. And yet she loved him, unconditionally, irrationally. Must be pheromones or something, Felix always told himself.

Two years ago, he had dragged her to Dreamfield for a job. A shit job, but it paid far better than anything he had been able to land before. She went without a fuss. She even pretended to like it in Dreamfield. But there was no skirting the Black-Eyed Truth: they were outsiders in this place and always would be.

There was a welcome sign on the one-way street that led into Dreamfield. The subtitle of the sign read: "Rated One of the Top Ten Friendliest Towns in Amerika." Translation: If you were born and raised in Dreamfield, god bless you; if you were born and raised somewhere else, fuck you.

"How much do you think a contact lens weighs?" asked Felix as he unscrewed one side of a case.

Helen stuck her feet in the air and wiggled her toes. "Dunno. How much does a housefly weigh? Does a contact lens weigh more than a housefly?"

He fished a lens from the case and put it in his palm to clean it. His fingers tensed and his hand buckled. "I think my contact lenses weigh 40 pounds. They're disposables. No joke, honey. I step on the scale, and it says 160 lbs. I step off, put my contacts in, step back on, and it says 200 lbs. That's 20 pounds per contact lens. I'm sure of it. I've stepped on and off the scale, like, a million times. It's like wearing dumbbells in my eyes.

And yet my head doesn't hang. I have a strong neck."

Sighing, she rolled over onto her back. "You have a strong neck," she echoed.

"That's what I say about it."

"You're full of shit, baby."

"I'm not full of anything but slippery tidbits." He clucked his tongue. "I'm just a storyteller."

"Nobody likes storytellers—especially when they call themselves storytellers. You're a ————, anyway. Now go to work." She spread her legs and traced the outline of her pubic hair. "Don't forget to give me a kiss goodbye."

18

Felix Soandso Goes Home

. . . A black 1978 Camaro Z28 drove by. Black blasts of smoke pumped from its exhaust in synch with the distorted electronic bass that made the tinted windows vibrate and threaten to shatter at any moment. An onlooker felt the bass in her guts so deeply she had to pause and massage her stomach back to health. The car seemed to have been assaulted by a hail of bricks, but it kept on trucking, so to speak, and then it took a right turn and vanished into a cornfield . . .

. . . A black and white Motorola TV with rabbit ears bound in crinkled tinfoil—somebody left it on the roadside. "The Rifleman" was on. The TV was not plugged in . . .

. . . He opened the door and stepped outside . . . into a cloud of swinefunk. Wincing, he covered his nose with a handkerchief.

He had not walked two blocks down Main Street when he heard somebody shout his name: "Hey you fuckin' soandso! Heads up you fuckin' faggot!" He looked over his shoulder to see who it was.

A container of worms struck him in the face. He fell over, gagging on dirt.

"Ha-ha-ha-ha-ha-ha-ha-ha-ha-ha-ha-ha-ha-ha-ha," dopplered the voices . . .

. . . "There's a TV out there in the street," Felix said, entering the bedroom. He took off his coat and dropped it on the floor. "It has rabbit ears. You don't see many TVs like that one anymore."

Helen stepped out of the bathroom in a robe. "Is it me or is it five o'clock already? Didn't you just leave two minutes ago? What's on your chin?"

Felix licked the butt of his palm and wiped off the dirt. "Nothing."

"You got some over there, too. What is that?"

"I don't know." He wiped his jaw.

"You missed a spot." Helen pointed at his ear. "What is that stuff?"

"Dirt." He licked his fingertips and pinched his ear lobe. "Somebody threw dirt at me."

"What, like, a clump of dirt?"

"Not exactly." He walked past her into the bathroom and inspected his face in the mirror. "It was a container of worms. Do I have any worms on my face?"

"Not that I can see."

He walked back into the bedroom. Helen looked at him sympathetically.

"I don't think I'm going to work today," he said, sitting on the bed with a deep sigh.

"Go to work," said Helen.

"I have a sick day coming, I think. Don't we all?"

"Go to work."

"They won't even miss me. They probably won't even know I'm not there. They'd probably prefer it if I didn't go in. Nobody likes me. Nobody likes some asshole who gets worms thrown at him."

"Go to work."

"All right." He stood, picked up his coat and put it back on. "But I'm not going to the festival this afternoon."

"You're going to the festival."

"I don't want to. I don't fit in. I don't have anything to say to these people. What do you say to them?"

"You say hello. You say wow what a nice day it is. You say boy oh boy that sure is a good-looking truck. You say hey where the heck you get that truck? You say life's a bitch and then you marry one. Then you say something about the weather again. You know what you say."

"I don't like saying those things."

"Do it."

"Goddamn it. I have to do everything."

Helen scratched the sharp arch of her eyebrow to show her husband that he had dirt on his eyebrow. He didn't get the message. Helen said, "Look, I know you don't want to go. I don't want to go. But if we're going to live here, we need to make an effort. We've discussed this. All right?"

"Yeah yeah yeah."

Before he left again, she gave him a hug, then wet her finger and cleaned his eyebrow in three strong, careful strokes.

Contes Cruelles

A thousand plateaus away from Dreamfield, Indiana, a woman ordered another woman to cut off a man's lips. Mascara-caked eyes screamed above a slash of duct tape.

"Do it with a paper cutter. Put him on his stomach and rest his chin on the grid and stretch out his lips and slice them off like the unseemly white edges of a Polaroid. Lips serve no real purpose anyhow other than to keep the teeth warm at night. Smiles and frowns are rawhide clichés—people have been smiling and frowning since the dawn of man. It's time for teeth to come out of the closet, in a manner of speaking, and let the sunshine in."

"No," said the woman squarely.

The other woman said, "Fine. Here." She handed her a pair of scissors. "I'll hold his head." She grabbed the tail of a mullet and yanked backwards.

The woman regarded the scissors. They didn't look sharp enough. They looked, in fact, as if they had been purposely dulled, or in any case mishandled and overused; nicks, scratches and dings ran the length of the blades. She knew better than to say no twice, though. Lives were at stake.

"That's enough," said the other woman. "Cut off his lips and put them in a jar. Then we can get on with the business of existence."

Muffled cry. Muffled panting. Muffled shriek.

She yanked off the duct tape. Another shriek, this one clear and loud and hot.

She dropped the scissors on the floor. The man didn't have any lips. Blood spurted from the lesions where his lips were supposed to be.

"Shoot," said the woman.

The other woman gestured at the duct tape with her chin. The woman looked at it. Two ugly, smiling worms of flesh punctuated its underside. The woman squinted, studying the ripped off lips like an algebra equation.

Between howls of pain, the man sucked air and blood and spit through two tall rows of exposed teeth. He choked. He gurgled.

The other woman said, "I slathered the tape with an acidic adhesive. Home remedy. You could glue the tip of an elephant's trunk to a bridge and let it hang there no problem with this stuff. Of course, the trunk would eventually tear apart and the elephant would plummet into the river below, exploding like a barrel of slime on the rocks."

"That's not a pleasant image," said the woman.

The man screamed so hard one of his nostrils turned inside out and blew out of his nose and hung into his goatee like the finger of a rubber glove.

The other woman ran fingers through shiny blonde hair and rearranged her belt buckle. "Unpleasant imagery—the definition of modern love . . ."

Second Theory of Ultraviolence

See chapter 19. Additionally . . .

Reactions to the more formidable acts of insurgency have been displaced by heated debates concerning the roundabout ways in which "feelers" have been used to indoctrinate a new strain of arithmetic, particularly in the branches of algebra and advanced geometry. Originally mathematicians thought they had things down pat. Now this. I wonder if—

sheriff uses his badge as a throwing star and throws it at a gunslinger instead of drawing his pistol in a duel and the badge nicks the gunslinger's jaw like the quick stroke of a razorblade and that makes him mad he fires his six-shooter onetwothreefourfivesix misses every time by a ridiculously wide margin and that pisses off the sheriff goddamnit who now unearths a stash of authentic Japanese Havoc and Air Claw and Typhoon throwing stars with certain enhanced hydraulic pro-perties and additional electro-technologized huzzah that stick in the gunslinger like darts in clay and set him on fire and tear through his flesh searing scorching exploding limbs and bubble gum brains spatter of gore against the canvas of life at which point the sheriff reminds everybody not to fuck with him and go about their chores lest he relieve them of their precocious innards. At the end of the street, a getaway car with a racing stripe down the hood makes roadkill out of a pedestrian. The pedestrian whispers an unassuming poem before bleeding out. It goes like this: . . .

—but sometimes one has to renegotiate terms, so to speak, if only to quell the sensation of existential dread that effectuates from an overdose of plus, minus, multiplication and division signs. Cartesian logic inevitably fails. All that remains are clockwork men, pregnant cartoons, and the technocapitalist media that define their inter(active)dictions . . .

Tanning Saloon

Sunday. 2:15 p.m. The sermon ended and church was officially dismissed. Winded, the pastor collapsed onstage and sponged sweat from his brow, neck and armpits with a Shamwow!® as the congregation flooded into the street and scuffled down the block *en masse* to the tanning saloon.

Before long, a line coiled around Main Street, Crazy Woman Crick Avenue, Logan's Run Boulevard, Crittersville Road . . .

Pale with repentance, the congregation waited patiently to enter the saloon, mumbling about warlocks and witchery and pro-choice, anti-gun, non-evangelical, neo-bourgeois, pro-intellectual demonology.

Creak of saloon doors.

Inside a bartender wearing suspenders, a blue dress shirt with white cuffs, and a wingtip mustache dished out shots of tequila, hammering the shots into the bar counter before serving them. Dreamfielders gobbled packets of salt, drank their portions, and chased them with thin slices of key lime pie that they shoveled into their mouths with plastic forks. Then they took off their clothes and removed their girdles, rolls of fat spilling to the knees, and filed into a HEX booth. Fizz of electricity. In a matter of seconds, the purple light turned their white bodies into bright orange blobs. They exited the HEX, put on their girdles and clothes, paid a doorman for the public service, and walked back outside, temporarily blinded by the sun, temporarily overwhelmed by the vastness of the blue sky, then adjusting, acclimatizing, forgetting . . . ready to face the clockwork of the week ahead.

Creak of saloon doors.

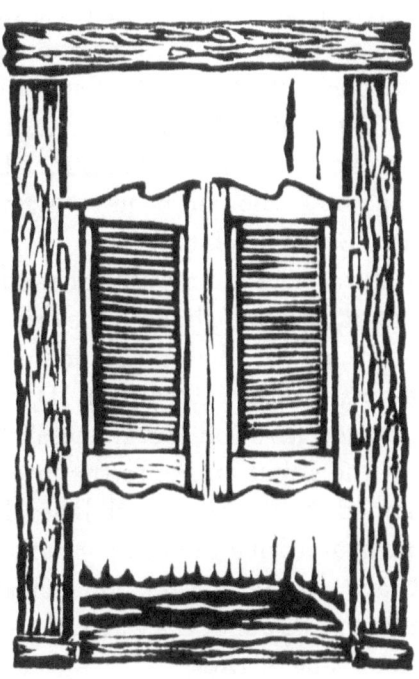

The Farmer's Revenge

Darin Rosengarter hopped onto the banana seat of a three-speed Huffy and started to ride it around the cul-de-sac. He ran over a caterpillar. He ran over an inflatable duck. He ran over the neighbor's dog. The neighbor stormed outside, shook a fist at the boy, and threw a Chia Pet at him. Darin dodged it, did another revolution, and ran over the Chia Pet. Then he ran over the neighbor's boy, who had been racing around the cul-de-sac in a Green Machine.

An agricultural tractor ran over Darin Rosengarter. "Get that shit outta here!" shouted the driver from his banana seat. He crouched atop the bloated, towering vehicle like an ant on a watermelon. "Dark clouds're on the way, Seersucker! God's my witness!" The tractor roared down the street and onto the interstate at 7 mph. It spanned the length of both lanes, holding up traffic behind it, and driving oncoming traffic into fields of wheat, beans and sunflowers. Some oldsters failed to get their lead sleds out of the way and were crushed by the tractor's galactic tires.

Two miles down the road, the festival was just getting underway on the fairground by the lake. They held festivals there twice a month. During the winter, they held them inside, alternating between the Moose Lodge, the Elks Lodge, the Eagles Lodge, the Beavers Lodge, the Deer Lodge, the Knights of Indianapolis Lodge, the White Lodge . . .

Cranes lowered supersonic speedboats into the water for a cannonball run around a track demarcated by blowup sexdoll buoys. Oscar Mayer hot dog stands outnumbered port-a-johns three to one. Bikers smoked rollies. Garage bands played Nugent and Thorogood and Brooks and hundreds of air guitarists and air drummers and air front men mimicked them. Children threw handfuls of mud at unsuspecting ducks. Old, ruddy-cheeked men in tasseled shoes compared the length, breadth and design of their tassels. "I love people!" hollered a drunk clown. A policeman tackled a streaker. Somebody served a customer a cup of oil instead of a cold beer. Horde of tents. Arboreal dearth. Pigshit in every sinus. The ducks revolted, attacking the children with uninhibited beaks. Balloons popped as darts struck the corkboards. Carousel. Ferris wheel. 4-H clubbers and boy scouts did a light-hearted dance of death. Beyond the curve, a housewife daydreamed of gunmetal sunsets and mechanical birds. "Given the opportunity," added the clown, "it's always better to show than to tell. First rule of metaphysics."

Billy Seersucker paced back and forth near a plastic orange palm tree, preparing to rip an alligator in half. He had shot the beast first and had it stuffed so that it wouldn't try to eat him. His taxidermist vouched for him.

"I went like this!" chirped the taxidermist, making a sharp stuffing motion with his arm. He repeated the motion over and over as the audience idly inhaled large wisps of cotton candy.

Billy Seersucker wore a gray and pink striped seersucker suit with bleached white saddle shoes and button-down shirt and no tie. He tipped his straw skimmer hat chronically, as if addicted to the rim. His grin was too big and too white.

"This is nothing, folks," said Seersucker. "A waste of time, really. Pointless, really. But when a man dares me to do something, I do it, goddamn it. This Bud's for you, fella." He pointed at somebody in the audience.

He hoisted the alligator over his head and ripped it in half. The taxidermist had stuffed it with goosefeathers, superballs and hard candy, all of which exploded into the sky . . .

The audience fell on the candy in a fit of akrasia.

Seersucker threw the two halves of the alligator aside, tipped his hat, blew feathers from his nose, tipped his hat, smacked a bouncing superball out of the way, tipped his hat, and said, "Child's play! Is this really what you dumbasses wanna see? Enough monkey business, I say. Somebody give me a building. An outhouse, for the love of God. I'll press it over my head and treat it like a sheet of paper. I'll do it!"

"Seersucker!"

The ripper cocked his head.

The farmer ran over a beer tent and parked the tractor atop the Third Financial Bank tent. Fat people screamed. The farmer dismounted and slid down one of the tractor's arms. He hit the ground too hard and fell down. He got up. He said, "Seersucker!"

Billy Seersucker shielded his eyes and waved a limp, perfunctory hand.

Gripping a tire iron, the farmer approached his nemesis, kicking akrasiacs out of the way with shit-stained boots. As he got nearer, he pointed at Seersucker with the tire iron. "You killed my hog! You killed my damned prize hog! Hog killer!"

Seersucker still wasn't sure if the farmer was yelling at him. He didn't recognize the farmer. He glanced around and tipped his hat a few times to gain wits and bearings. Not until the farmer was within a few yards did he realize the score.

Nearby, a revving of cars preceded exclamations of *arriba* and *undulay* . . .

Nostalgia for Unruffled Feathers

Street fighters in the form of two mutant scorpions attack one another atop an undulating bed of red ants that threatens to devour the arachnids at any moment. But they don't. The scorpions bite one another, sting one another, tear one another's tails and legs and claws off, reducing themselves to mere thumbs of foiled aggression. And light fades from their eye stalks in the dust of dawn . . . Recollect what it used to be like before the storm. Impossible. The storm hits—veins of electricity illuminate the sky, raindrops and hail and worms and frogs explode against the pavement, *abrazo* of musclebound clouds, a cow gallops across the road, cars swerve, cars crash, plumes of fire stand in the darkness, mangled homeowners screech, they claw out of the wreckages like zombies from the grave, dragging slick pieces of themselves by shoestrings, gaping holes and flailing tentacles unbound, a foundry of mass market gore—these images are forever nailed into the doors of perception. Despite herculean efforts, they cannot be erased . . . The future flickers like childhood and dares onlookers to reclaim it.

24

The Farmer's Head

It came apart like sun-dried burlap. The soft interior seemed to vaporize. Only diaphanous shreds remained, as if somebody had clumsily peeled the head open with razorsharp claws. Nonetheless the farmer's body continued to move forward and lunged at Billy Seersucker with the tire iron. It struck him again and again, growing weaker with each blow, until the farmer's lower half dropped the tire iron, ambled towards the lake in a drunken zigzag, and fell onto its chest, twitching.

"What the heck?" said Billy Seersucker, whose head came apart like sun-dried burlap . . .

This Is What Happened Next

In the Psyche: a collective breakdown/breakthrough. Then a quick devolution into animalistic impulsiveness and beyond-the-word-is-chaos exploits.

Nobody knew what happened and everybody overreacted, bawling, gesticulating, darting to and fro like birds on wires, wondering just what they had seen . . . They had seen two heads explode. They knew that. Maybe . . .

Questions tore across the thin, fevered skin of consciousness as the Boat filled with Water . . .

. . . those two fellas? . . .

. . . noises, gunshots or fireworks? . . .

. . . god's green arf . . .

. . . animatronic hombres? . . .

. . . if I die right here? . . .

. . . flicker . . .

. . . gizzard, ventriculus, gastric mill, gigerium . . .

. . . shinola, sandbugswarm . . .

. . . in fronta my eyes? . . .

. . . Seersucker an illusionist? . . .

. . . popsicle sticks interacting with . . .

. . . tear shit up . . .

. . . up in flames? . . .

. . . upside down . . .

. . . death photos coil from the Polaroid

. . . grinning slit . . .

. . . strangers of the mustache, the dark glass? . . .

. . . slosh of disembowelment . . .

. . . flutter of wrens across the lake surface . . .

. . . heck? . . .

. . . ??? . . .

(Fusillade of sonic booms. Exuent ONE HUNDRED DREAMFIELDERS *from the playhouse.)*

Exclamations of *arriba* and *undulay* funneled into incoherent squelches of power, authority, and wild purposelessness. *(Dance. And exeunt again.)*

26

Port-a-John

"What'n the heck?" Vaughn Peters grumbled. The port-a-john creaked and shuddered with all the commotion. Sounded like the Alpha and the Omega got in a brawl. He would have to finish later, although not at home—never at home. Taking dumps in public accommodations was, aside from working at the factory, lifting weights at the gym, and sometimes playing with his kids, his chief MO. Every dump was an insignia of identity. The more he dumped, the bigger he grew, so to speak. That he couldn't continue to grow bigger at this time didn't please him. He stood and wiped himself. It was dirty. He cursed and continued to wipe himself until he had clogged the toilet hole with TP, then pulled up and buckled his jeans, wiped his hands off on his sleeves, threw open the door of the port-a-john, and blustered outside.

Tinny suction noise . . . Images of the War rushed back to him. He saw the melting faces. He saw the raw body parts strewn across the grass. He saw the towering piles of naked corpses. He saw the dread and the desperation in his soul that underlined the inevitability of death and nothingness . . .

He saw a man with a black mustache and gold-rimmed, mirror-red sunglasses. The man stood before him, smiling like a shadow. If he reached out, he could almost stroke the darkness . . .

At Vaughn Peters' funeral, his family drank cold beers and sang twangy Linda Ronstadt and Kenny Rogers ballads.

27

Five Bloodslides

In 20XX, after much debate, they finally turned the name of the soap opera *As the World Turns* to *The World Has Turned to Celluloid*, which subsequently assimilated all of the other remaining soap operas (e.g., *One Life to Live*, *The Young and the Restless*, *All My Children*, etc.). Thus every mainstream channel between the times of 1 and 4 p.m. featured the same episode with the same major and minor characters, foremost among them the eye-in-the-sky patriarch, Viktor Kiriakis, played by Jennifer Aniston's father, John "Like the Biblical Character" Aniston. Appropriately, the opening scene of the debut episode of *The World Has Turned to Celluloid* features a bloodslide induced by the tearing in half of a Kiriakisian bastard who discharged far more blood than humanly possible. There was no motive for the tearing in half of this young man. Nor did viewers have the opportunity to see the murderer (he wore a brown paper bag over his head). Nor was the apprehension and disclosure of the murderer pursued in the narrative of the show. After the eight minute bloodslide, the show abruptly faded out and faded in to a sex scene between two teenage girls who had had it up to here with the juvenile tomfoolery and inexperience of teenage boys. This piece of context, however, was not made available until much later, when the audience least expected it. Up to that point, the girls simply performed inscrutable sexual acts upon one another.

Celluloid makes more noise than the cruel bark of reality. If you heat celluloid over a flame, it emits evil electric hisses as spoonfuls of the substance drip onto the warm earth . . .

Three blocks from the festival's east end, a boy knelt down on the sidewalk to get a closer look at a celluloid stain on the pavement. It looked like this:

> *(Chesty blonde in fishnet tights strides into the boxing ring and does two revolutions holding over her head a poster board with an image of the celluloid stain on it, wowing spectators.)*

The boy couldn't decide if the stain was shaped like a gnu facing west or a headshot of his father in a bad mood. He was still trying to decide when a sudden, raging bloodslide washed over him and carried his body into a cornfield.

Shortly thereafter, a bloodslide accosted an elderly couple taking a walk by the lake. They had been strolling down a stretch of path that led around the outskirts of a rare agglomeration of trees when the bloodslide leapt out of the trees and knocked them into the water. They couldn't swim, and they drowned in trillions of angry corpuscles.

Shortly before this incident, a retiree poured himself a cup of coffee, smelled the coffee, sipped it, sighed, and glanced out the front window of his house. He lived on a golf course, just west of the 12th hole's green. It was a decent, well-groomed course, although flat, and he could clearly see the cinderblock walls of Wal-Mart and Menards in the distance, standing at attention like conjoined twins. He noticed something on the tee. Not a man. Not an animal. More like a . . . blot. A big blot. Dark. Undulating. Getting bigger.

Flowing down the fairway . . .

He spilled his coffee. He lurched outside in pajamas and flip-flops.

Tall and long as an ocean liner, the bloodslide rumbled by the retiree in slow motion. He watched it go, awe-struck, shielding his eyes from froth and spatter. After it had passed, he hopped in a golf cart and began to chase it. But he crashed the golf cart in a sand trap on the 17th hole and couldn't get it going again. Black wheels spun in white sand.

A bloodslide collapsed on the festival. Only a few Dreamfielders drowned. The rest swam home, to church, or to Wal-Mart.

On Armstrong Street, another bloodslide collided with a gust of celluloid.

The result was a Big Budget blockbuster.

28

A Shoe Store Named Footland

Soft ambient music. Elastic grins. Idle chatter. Neutral shades of color.

The salesman's bald spot seemed like, at any moment, it might yawn open and digest the scraps of hair that lingered on the periphery of his head. Ronald Ronman stared at it as the salesman, kneeling on polyester slacks, measured his foot and strung laces into a pair of black wingtips. The bald spot intimidated him. Still, he felt pretty good. Relaxed. He liked the music in Footland. It was soporific. And the leather chair he sat in felt so comfortable, as if it had been tailor-made for his ass and spine. There was a pleasant smell in the shoe store, too. Sandalwood. Somebody had lit incense. Not the cheap stuff either. This was kind incense—not too strong or abrasive, no induction of paranoia, and every time he inhaled, slowly, deeply, his sinuses opened wider and wider.

His eyelids grew heavy.

"Rumor has it that the Florsheim Lexington is an unreliable, unremarkable piece of hardware," said the salesman, slipping on and tying the unit. He squeezed his customer's foot reassuringly and looked up into his eyes. "But I can promise you this, Mr. Ronman: if you give this little number a chance, it'll quickly become your favorite shoe."

Ronald smiled as his head dipped towards his shoulder like a drinking bird and sleep engulfed him.

A tractor crashed through the window as if catapulted from across the street.

The salesman sprung to his feet and said, "Holy fuuuuuuuuuuuuck!" The tractor hit him squarely. It hit another unsuspecting salesman, two customers, three assistant sales managers and a mannequin—all of whom exploded, to varying degrees, when the tractor sandwiched them into a brick wall.

Ronald Ronman's heart jumped into his mouth. He flew backwards out of the chair and somersaulted into a pyramid of shoe boxes. He stood . . . too quickly. Blood rushed to his head and he lost balance and fell down. He stood again. Hot spots swam like amoebas across his screen of vision as he struggled to bring the scene into focus. Was he dreaming? He didn't know. Where was he? He didn't know. Who was he? Ronald Ronman. What did he see?

This is what he saw: a man, dark, grinning, sinewy and angular—a praying mantis on its hind legs. He lingered in the window, tall and resolute, silhouette flickering as his head eclipsed the sun.

Solarized Crow's Nest POV

LONG RANGE DOWN-ANGLE SHOT on a woman running across an empty street. She's crying. She's wearing a thin, flower-patterned sun dress. No shoes. No hat. No makeup from what we can tell at this distance. Medium-length brunette hair. Marginal breasts. Her shoulders are pointed but not in a way that suggests anorexia. Good skin—olive-toned without discernable moles or unseemly patches of hair.

Delicate yet strong and capable extremities.

And yet she is out of control. Broken. She isn't running in a straight line, and she doesn't appear to be running anywhere in particular.

A long car enters the page . . . an old, dirty, white Chrysler Le-Baron convertible with a burgundy Naugahyde interior. There are four men in it. Jet black hair. Mustaches. Blood red fighter pilot sunglasses. White suits, black shirts, gold chains . . . The car putters after the woman for a few beats, then accelerates and runs her over. She gets up and hobbles in the other direction. The car does a leisurely U-turn and runs her over again, breaking her legs. She crawls away. The car does another U-turn and runs her over again, then backs over her, then drives forward over her, crunching her frail bones . . . She lies still, face-down, the skirt of her dress cast onto her back, exposing her . . . The car idles. None of its occupants look over their shoulders or in the rear view mirrors to see what they have done. They stare forward. Then a man in the back seat puts a harmonica to his lips . . . POV CREEPS BACKWARDS, ascending into the sky, and the LeBaron peels away, off-page, in a swell of dirt and dust.

Last line of the chapter—a quotation—a string of dialogue—a dark, gravely voice-over with a faint air of empathy and caring: . . . "We must first understand violence before we can control it."

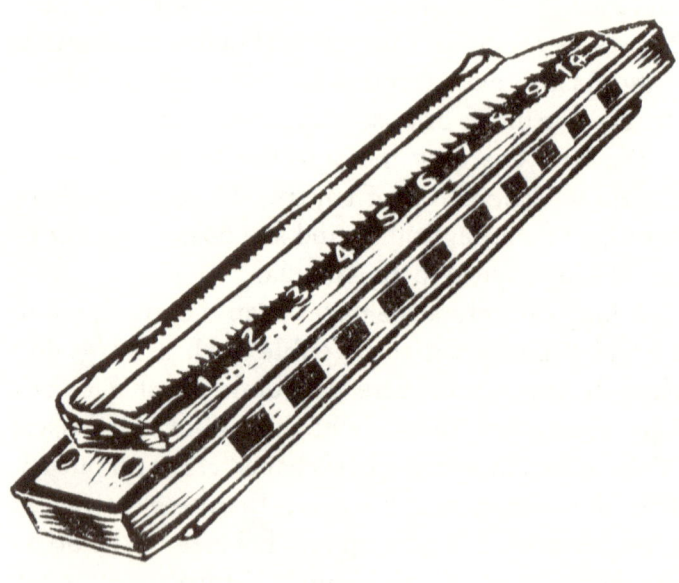

Samson Thataway & The Fuming Garcias

This is a book about the telling of ultraviolent deeds. No deed can be done without a telling to distinguish its contours. Narrative as the ember of the nightmare of life.

Sound of a spray bottle . . .

The first thing they did was raid a dog food repository situated a mile outside of Dreamfield's city limits. They shot all of the factory workers, ate all of the dog food, and beat up all of the dogs. They did the same thing to a Walgreens up the street, only they killed cashiers, ate candy, and beat up the pharmacist and the photo technician. They proceeded in this fashion down Main Street, shitstorming a hair salon, a fryhouse, a fire station, a movie theater, another hair salon, another fryhouse, another hair salon, a Dairy Queen . . . until Main Street ended and they found themselves parked in front of a Carousel.

There were ten cars, softly revving, vintage LeBaron convertibles with red interiors, each of them occupied by four men, two in front, two in back. All but one of the men looked more or less the same—born of Leonean-Amerikan descent with an indecipherable aura of the extreme Guido. Trademark white Montana suits accentuated their luminescent red sunglasses and shoepolish black mustaches. Their movements were vaguely robotic, yet not necessarily inhuman; as they filed out of the LeBarons and slammed the doors, they surveyed the festival methodically, scanning the territory with calculated, birdlike gestures of the head. Knuckles cracked.

When they became excited, or angry, or bloodthirsty, or altogether psychotic, or, in some cases, fiendishly apathetic—their sunglasses glowed with greater intensity. Occasionally the lenses caught fire.

The last figure to exit a LeBaron didn't look like the others. He wore all black—black cowboy boots, black jeans, black belt with big black buckle, black shirt, black gloves, black leather jacket, black aviator sunglasses— and he had a well-groomed black pompadour hairdo that might have been a wig. It looked flimsy, off-center and poorly applied, as if the slightest wind might topple it. And yet the hairdo stayed in place; not a follicle stepped out of rank. All this blackness was offset by the skin of his face, deathly pallid, caked in a layer of cheap white makeup.

He did not own a mustache.

He carried a half gallon spray bottle of computer cleaner everywhere he went.

Not coincidentally, the difference in appearance between this man and his companions was the first thing he brought to light, announcing, "I'm not like the others!" although one onlooker wondered if, by "others," he meant in comparison to the other strangers or to people in general. At any rate, that was the first thing he said.

The second thing he said was: "If they exist, kill 'em."
Gore.

. . . After the initial wave of bloodshed, the man strode into the middle of the ramparts to address the dead, the moribund, and the soon-to-be moribund and dead as his companions reloaded Jurassic magnums. "They call me Samson Thataway," he intoned, arranging long limbs in a dramatic power-stance. As always, sunlight slipped behind his hairdo when he spoke, leaving his body in shadow. "I suck the meat out of life and crap it into a dirty ashtray. I was born on a Thursday. Mamma sold me to a man with a goat head for sixty cents. I grew up. I got fuckin' drunk and stoned and madder than a hornet in a shit factory. That's all she wrote."

He sprayed the corners of his mouth with the computer cleaner. Shudder of ecstasy. He licked his lips and indulged himself again. Countless years of spraying had rendered his lips two flattened, cooked maggots, and the skin that surrounded the lips was cracked, corroded, hideous—tundra of the flesh.

Tears of dried blood stained his anvil of chin.

"There you are," said Thataway, admiring the spray bottle, and spraying himself again. Satisfied, he chirped, "And now permit me to introduce my companions, the Fuming Garcias." He made a theatrical sweeping gesture with his arms. "Buyers beware—they do not emit fumes, and their real names are not Garcia. Moreover, they are neither clones nor brothers, even though they look almost exactly alike. I hand picked them myself. And yet the fact that so many men look almost exactly alike defies all notions of coincidence or causality. It is nothing less than impossible, you mink-livered, egg-swallowin' whores. I trust that each of you will exercise equal shares of deference as the Fuming Garcias wreak havoc from dawn's early light to twilight's last gleaming over the shithole you call home. They're a wild bunch."

Somebody complained about death throes. Somebody else shrieked, and died.

Samson Thataway sniffed something. He sniffed it again with more vigor and glanced over his shoulders at the Fuming Garcias. "Did somebody just eat an orange?" The Fuming Garcias looked at each other and shrugged. Thataway said, "I smell a goddamn orange." He sprayed himself. "I don't like that smell. But I don't blame whoever ate the orange. They're good for you. They taste nice. But you can't get that smell off of you. It takes days. I haven't eaten an orange since I was a young rascal. Real men eat . . ."

Rape Scene

The woman enjoys it. The men feel violated. They intend to sue the woman for crimes against masculinity. They intend to win.

They curl the sharp ends of their mustaches around mindful index fingers as the neon signs of Dreamfield's restaurants collectively flicker off.

32

Confusion's Company

Felix Soandso stepped on a clump of pigshit as he neared the entrance. He didn't notice until it was too late. He had just shined his shoes. Who had been out walking their pig? Who walked their pig and didn't clean up its feces? . . . Could have been anybody. Almost everyone he knew kept house swine in addition to ever-expanding crops of slaughterhouse pigs. He suspected one co-worker in particular. Rebecca Comanche. She brought her pig to work half the time, tethering it to the bike rack outside all day long except during lunch and on breaks when she came out to play with it. No sign of Wilbur now. Maybe Rebecca had it in her cubicle. Every now and then the boss allowed employees to keep such company.

As he cleaned off his shoe with a handkerchief, Felix tried not to breath through his nose, and he tried to stay positive—two efforts he made on a regular basis whenever he went outside, meaning he simply amped up the intensity with which he denied his nose and mind these negativities. As always, he focused on Helen, perhaps the only good thing in his life, aside from their new 50" HD TV, but harnessing inspiration from the TV was difficult to do unless he was watching it. What about Helen? Her smile. Her smell. Her stomach. The dimple at the summit of her ass crack. He loved that dimple. Genuinely. There was nothing sexual about it. Something about the dimple gave him hope; at the very least it provided comfort. He didn't know why. There was nothing special about it. It was a simple indentation of flesh, and not a very deep indentation at that. And yet it soothed him. Just the thought of it soothed him. He was soothed right now, imagining the dimple spreading across the leather skin of his shoe like a beautiful dermatosis.

"I love you, Felix," whispered the dimples in tangled unison. Their voices echoed away . . .

He put the dirty handkerchief in an ash can and went inside. He ducked left and speedwalked to the restroom to wash his hands.

He froze in the doorway, jarred by the sight and smell of the pig.

Somebody had tied the round, pink beast to a sink pipe by a yellow leash. It wore a collar studded with spikes and its hind legs stood in a small pool of what was ostensibly its own urine.

The pig didn't look familiar. It wasn't Wilbur anyway.

Felix washed his hands, peering askance at the pig. The pig watched him with upraised snout and wide, admonitory eyes. It appeared to be on the verge of scolding him. He expected the invective to begin any second.

He turned off the faucet, dried his hands, and sidled up to a urinal. He unzipped his pants.

He looked over his shoulder. The pig had rearranged itself so that it could stare at him directly. The same haughty, derisive expression punctuated its fat head.

He couldn't go. He gripped the locket around his neck. Opened it. The picture inside looked different. It was him. Same blank, unassuming expression. But different, somehow.

He zipped up his pants and left the restroom.

On the way to his desk, co-workers delivered him the same confused glances he received every morning, as if it were his first day, or they were surprised he hadn't been fired, or he was trespassing on private property. But there was something strange about the way they regarded him today. He couldn't put his finger on it, and it irked him more than the pig that gave him stagefright. Confusion wasn't the only emotion on their faces. It had company. Without close inspection, though, he couldn't gauge the disposition of that company, and he didn't want to call attention to himself.

He disavowed the notion, reminding himself how deeply and intricately disavowal factored into the purview of every social being, allowing one to compensate for the many ways in which one *fails* on a daily basis. Without disavowal, society would timelapse into obscurity.

His desk adjoined the desk of Walter Spittmocker at the rear so that they faced one another. Every employee had been paired up and situated in the same way. Invariably the pairings consisted of two employees who, based on various diagnostic and psychological evaluations, weren't predisposed to friendship, which would preclude them from deviating from work-related business to the business of small talk.

Felix always made small talk.

It said a lot for him, he thought. Walter Spittmocker was a sociopath . . . or something. He appeared normal enough—not bad-looking, not poorly dressed, not too fat, not too bald, no body odor, neither loud nor outspoken . . . Felix couldn't stand him. Two reasons. His eyes were terminally uncrossed, which is to say, each eye peered out of its farthest corner, as if the irises were allergic to one another, or better yet, magnetically opposed to one another, creating an effect that suggested something altogether inhuman, and yet Walter claimed to have 20/20 vision. This may or may not have been Walter's fault. Whatever the case, in and of themselves, the eyes didn't merit annoyance or enmity. Coupled with his personality, however, they beckoned Felix's disdain. Walter had what Felix could only describe as an acausal personality. Responses and comments frequently didn't correspond with questions and remarks that had been put to him. He blurted random information. He became happy when he should have been sad, or anxious, or angry. Then, suddenly, for as long as a half hour, his eyes would un-uncross and he would conduct himself in an impeccably causal fashion, talking to Felix as if they were good friends. Irked, Felix fended off his gregarious advances, and the moment he decided that, this time, maybe Walter had turned over a new leaf for the long haul, Walter's eyes sprung back to their posts and he slipped into Uncanniness again, without provocation. Was he malicious, tactical, evil? Or was he just a weirdo? No way to tell what made him tick.

Some days Felix elected to give Walter the silent treatment from beginning to end. Other days he spoke to Walter despite Walter and despite his own feelings towards him.

This was an other day.

He sat down. "Good morning."

Walter got up and walked away. He came back five minutes later with a cup of coffee. He took a sip and dumped the rest in a trash bin. He sat back down.

"That reminds me of a cup of coffee I once drank," said Felix, arranging and rearranging papers, pens and file folders on his desk. "I didn't like the taste of it, so I threw it out. There was a man who saw me do it. I don't know if he brewed the coffee or if he knew who brewed the coffee. Perhaps his relatives had grown the beans. Anyway, he didn't like what I had done to the coffee. He tried to make a citizen's arrest. I wouldn't let him. So there was this big to-do. Lawyers and judges and reverends flocked to the scene. They called me names. They tried to take advantage of me. But I was able to evade them. In addition, I poured myself another cup of coffee and threw it out before taking a sip. I didn't even smell it. Everybody was flabbergasted. They didn't know what to do. They went away and never bothered me again. The end."

Walter cleared his throat. "You need to be more attentive to detail."

Felix looked at his co-worker excitedly. "What?"

"Details. Don't tell. Show."

"What's the difference?"

Walter sighed. He reached beneath his desk and produced a small, vintage RCA TV. He placed the TV in front of Felix. "Turn it on."

"This thing is *old*," he said. "How old is this thing?" He ran a finger across the screen, wiping off a line of black dust.

"Turn it on," Walter repeated.

Felix made a frog face and pulled out the knob.

Nothing but static. "I don't see anything," said Felix. "Wait."

He waited.

"I don't see anything."

Walter raised a fist . . .

The static cleared. Gray screen. Then a pale string of text squelched into view. The lettering was small. Felix had to squint to read it.

CHAPTER 29
Solarized Crow's Nest POV

The text looked naked. He wanted to cover it with something. With imagery.

He said it aloud. "Chapter 29. Chapter 29. Chapter 29. Chapter 29."

At the sound of his voice, static swallowed the text. Through the dull crackle, Felix heard a crow squawk.

Walter turned off the TV and put it back under his desk. "I'm so sorry," he said, lips quivering. "This is what happens next." Cords popped onto Walter's neck. His eyelids fluttered as if he might faint. He got up again, fell to his knees, yelled something, whispered something, and crawled towards a water cooler.

Felix shuddered. He turned his head slowly and looked behind him.

No question about it now. Confusion's company had exposed itself.

Memento Mori Daguerreotypes

A man washed up on a bed of weeds. Dumb smile. Eyes half open. Bullet hole in temple—a bruised, leaking sphincter. Head set against an expanding pillow of red.

Cheap motel room with blood-spattered cinder block walls and wax paper bathmats.

Pasture of crossbow arrows bending in the wind. Flesh for soil.

Bear trap. Clenched shut. Leg stumps to the east. Head and arm stumps to the west. Torso mangled in the intricate jaws. North of the frame, the rim of a quiet gutter.

Perforated bodies drool from the rusted carriages of a Ferris wheel, the acrylic horses of a Carousel. Gruesome physical incarnations of Hobbesian ideology.

Corroded bodies in the mud. They have been robbed of their faces—no ears, no noses, no eyes or mouths. Identity as a smooth square of skin.

Overturned NASCAR vehicles.

Cosmic rendering of the circles of Dante's *Inferno*. The rednecks torture the Italians with neomedieval machinery. In *Purgatorio* and *Paradiso*, the rednecks smoke Camels and sip Mad Dog from crystal snouts.

Daguerreotype of a daguerreotype of a daguerreotype of a daguerreotype of a numb fisherman who has accidentally chased his line into the water and eaten his own bait. Close-up of a hooked lip.

A plaid suit torn to shreds. Horrific litter of fabric. The strangers loom over the carnage in a semi-circle. Sunlight shines through the cracks of their silhouettes.

Los hombres oscuros.

A sky camel and a dark horse racing down Main Street. The camel's gait outstretches the horse's by thirty feet.

The still shot treads water in slow motion . . .

34

Monty Python's "Salad Days" (1971), Directed by Sam Peckinpah

In this short video, the cast gets together on a "simply super day" to play tennis. The men wear white pants, striped suit coats and ties, and straw boater hats. The women wear floppy, flowery sunhats and sundresses. Everybody is happy and excited to get some exercise. One gentleman exclaims, "I say, anyone for tennis?" and brandishes a wooden racquet. "Oh super! What fun!" pipe the others. Another gentleman responds, "I say, Lionel, catch," and throws a tennis ball at him.

The ball strikes Lionel in the face and his nose explodes. Blood exits in hideous squirts.

Aggrieved, Lionel throws his racquet aside. It strikes a woman in the stomach, mauling her. Blood exits in hideous squirts.

Losing balance, the woman tries to steady herself by grabbing onto a man's arm. She tears his arm off. Blood exits in hideous squirts.

The man with one arm stumbles over to a white piano where John Cleese is playing a happy song. He slams the keyboard cover onto Cleese's hands and severs them. Blood exits in hideous squirts.

Screaming woman.

Slow motion. Blood exits in hideous squirts from Cleese's wrists. Blood urinates on the overturned piano.

Slower motion. Screaming woman.

A man impaled by a long ladder howls and stumbles over the remains of the "simply super day."

35

Third Theory of Ultraviolence

They burned off his eyelids with nitrocellulose.

And Dr. Ludavico, baring a geometry of perception, cocked his head and said, "I viddy. I viddy horrorshow."

The Hallucinatory Chemistry of Panic

Felix loomed over her body. He couldn't believe it was her. He had only seen the dead bodies of strangers before. At funerals. Cremation was the tradition in his family. He didn't know how to feel. He didn't know what he felt. Everything. And nothing.

"That's her."

The triple-chinned coroner nodded gravely and covered her face with a sheet. "Postmortem rape kit indicates that the subject was not physically raped but may have been the subject of various male rape fantasies. Many women perform this function. Apologies, Mr. Soandso." A double-chinned police officer escorted Felix from the room. In the hallway, he said, "We'll need a formal statement, please."

Felix stared at the officer's badge. "The loud flame needs the quiet ember."

"Pardon me, sir?"

"Nothing."

The policeman took out a pen and pad of paper. "Now then. Tell me what happened. Have you seen anything strange today? Anything out of the ordinary? Tell me what happened."

"Have I seen anything strange today? Strange? Are you kidding me?"

"Please refrain from that cynical tone, sir. I'm sorry for your loss. But death hardly merits a cynical tone."

Felix swore.

The policeman said he wasn't following the rules and threatened to arrest him. Felix said, "Have I seen anything strange today?"

"That's the question I asked. I'll ask it one more time. Have you seen anything strange to—?"

Felix punched the policeman in the stomach, losing his fist momentarily in a roll of fat. The policeman doubled over. "Strange!" Felix shouted. "Look at the goddamn TVs!"

He pointed at the ceiling. Rows of flatscreens ran the length of the hallway from one end to the other. Every TV featured the same story with the same footage regarding various "strangers on the loose."

Felix kicked the policeman in the balls, knocking him over.

A horde of multi-chinned policemen tackled Felix, rolled around on him for awhile until he stopped squirming and gesticulating, cuffed him, and dragged him out of the hospital.

In his cell, he felt the hallucinatory chemistry of panic. First stage: My wife is dead. Second stage: One day I'll be dead. Third stage: Life is a cruel joke, afterlife an illusory crutch.

Fourth stage: *Sic semper tyrannus.*

Carjack

In the semicircular, bubble-lighted entrance of the
Nameless One Screen Movie Theater, the Fuming
Garcias erected a giant pneumatic slingshot. They
loaded pickup trucks, RVs, school buses, fire engines,
squad cars into the slingshot and slung them across the
street. The vehicles demolished building after building.
Each act of demolition produced loud, villainous yips
of glee.

   An arbitrary Fuming Garcia carried a silver ghetto
blaster on his shoulder. The ghetto blaster blasted
Julian Lennon's "Too Late for Goodbyes" . . .

38

The Unpicked Brain

Ennui beleaguered Samson Thataway. Inevitably. He allowed himself to be apprehended, in a sense, on the condition that the police officers slapped cuffs onto their own wrists and piled into the trunk of their vehicle. He slipped into the patrol car and drove himself to the station. The Fuming Garcias followed in their polished LeBarons.

Police Chief Ollinger was dragged outside by his ears and ordered to remove the arresting officers from the trunk and knock them out with a bowling pin. Samson Thataway watched, dousing his mouth with a fresh dose of computer cleaner.

He told the chief to hit himself in the head as hard he could with the bowling pin. The chief refused.

Thataway's hairdo devoured the sun . . .

"Call a Talk Doctor!" howled Thataway in the waiting room of the police station. "The unpicked brain festers and swells! The unpicked brain explodes like a gremlin in the microwave!" He waited patiently for six seconds, then pulled a gun on the receptionist.

Gun Fetish

In slow motion, it takes two minutes to traverse the barrel of the .44 Magnum Colt Anaconda Hyperphallic Plus. This high velocity, single-action handgun glints and twinkles in the vast purple brilliance of the cosmos. Its chrome-coated frame is complimented by a mother-of-pearl Bisley grip that features an etching of a zombified Charleton Heston's bust. The sight of the gun seems not only to reify but to enhance and technologize masculinity. An epidemic of bulging tumescence sweeps across the theater. Bare boy-chests burst into flames of hair. Biceps and deltoids and gluts bulge and throb. Exodus. The streets ignite and overflow with bug-eyed, teeth-gnashing, cock-a-doodle-doodling beasts of the subhuman night . . .

A fingertip tightens on the trigger. It becomes clear that the fingernail has undergone an exquisite manicure—perfectly cut and filed into a soft curve, perfectly smooth texture, sans cuticle, sans blemish of any kind. Sound of a factory machine coming to life. Sound of quickening hydraulics and waking pistons set to a synthesizer. Songs of The Crystal Method . . . Then, as the hammer comes down on its mark, as the cylinder turns and the brass base of a bullet clanks into place: . . . *KA-tooooooozzzsh*.

An empty gold cartridge arcs out of the Anaconda and the bullet leaves the cannon. It looks like an aluminum fang and grows larger and sharper as it closes on its target.

Splat.

40

Spigot

The receptionist floundered backwards out of his seat through a glass window across the room into the bars of an empty holding cell. His body convulsed. He made several amphibious noises. Then he slumped over dead.

An open box of donuts crashed to the floor and decayed in fasttime . . .

Samson Thataway inhaled the smoke from the muzzle of the Anaconda, held it in, and exhaled a string of quick, thick rings. "That's some kind shit. Excuse me." He spun the carbine into its holster and flicked open the button on his shirt above his belt buckle. He reached in and extracted a fleshy spigot that appeared to stem from his navel. The spigot stiffened and discharged a swampy black-green substance, like bong resin. He let it drain. It took half a minute.

He put the spigot away, rebuttoned his shirt and said, "Too much man juice. Holy hell. Now where's that Talk Doctor?"

Bad Grief

Deputy McKinney addressed Felix as if he were a spokesman for protein powder. "There's all kinds of brands," he clarified. "Naturally, the question you want to be asking yourself is, what kind of brand is the best brand, and what kind is the best brand for you specifically?" He paused. "That's two questions." He walked over to a refrigerator and picked up a glass blending container. "Whichever brand you use, though, you gotta mix it up with some fruit and yogurt and shit so it tastes good? Best way to mix something is with a blender." He held up the container. "It doesn't really matter what you put in the blender first. Some people say that, anyway. I think it's best to put in some ice first? Ice'll make your shake nice and cold when it gets blended up?" He pushed the container against the ice dispenser. Ice cubes tumbled into the container . . . and onto the floor. He had forgotten to screw on the bottom. "Dang!" He put the container aside and scrambled to pick up the ice. He slipped on a cube and fell into the refrigerator; his head bounced off of the pink door. "Dang!" He clutched his head, slipped on another ice cube, and fell onto his back, knocking the wind out of him.

Felix turned over and closed his eyes.

Contrary to the shell-shocked onset of grief, what he felt now was pure and clean and hard and overpowering and excruciating and evil and torturous. And he was effectively insane.

He tried to focus. Failed. He tried to put his wits in order. Failed. He tried to regain control of the derailed freight train of his psyche. Failed, failed.

In a painful strobe of memory, she gave him a guided meditation. He used to get so anxious. The smallest things unnerved him. "Close your eyes," she said, "and know that you are loved. Focus on your third eye. Inhale. Exhale." Her fingers began on his face and jaw and neck, massaging the skin and bone, then systematically moved down his body, to his feet, his toes. "Let the blackness flow out of you. When you exhale, let the blackness run through your body and empty from your fingers and toes. When you inhale, there is only clean white light. Inhale, exhale. Inhale, exhale. Know that you are loved. I love you . . ."

"Dang," wheezed Deputy McKinney . . .

Samson: An Analysis of a Case of Hysteria

Deputy Bell leaned over to Deputy Garrett and said, "What's a Talk Doctor? Don't all doctors talk some?"

Samson Thataway ordered a squad of Fuming Garcias to relieve the officers in the room of their weapons, strip them naked, wrap their heads in duct tape, and plant them in the front yard of the police station.

Later . . .

"He keeps killin' the doctors," said Deputy Baker to Deputy Alias. "Every time I send one in there, he gets mad and kills 'em. We're almost out of 'em."

Deputy Alias flexed his jaw. "Sometimes bad things happen to doctors."

. . . Dr. Acton entered the holding cell. There was a pile of mangled therapists in white, blood-stained uniforms in the far corner. One therapist hung from a ceiling rafter by a Fisher Price stethoscope.

Samson Thataway sat in a foldout chair behind a card table in the middle of the cell. He looked like Elvis, pumped and steroidal, shrouded in black, on the fringe of an anabolic breakdown. His mouth frothed beneath enormous sunglasses. Computer cleaner laced with saliva dripped from his chin onto the table in long strands.

Thataway welcomed the doctor and gestured for him to sit in the empty foldout chair across the table. Dr. Acton tentatively obliged, placing his briefcase between his feet.

"What's in the briefcase?" chirped Thataway.

"Apropos," said Dr. Acton, framing his sharp, bearded face with thumbs and index fingers.

Thataway smirked. "I like you. I'm gonna let you live a little."

"Very well. Tell me about yourself."

"I can make myself bleed."

"I see."

"I'm serious. I'm always serious."

"I understand."

"I doubt it. But I can make myself bleed. Mentally."

"Mentally."

"Watch."

He closed his eyes and squeezed . . .

Nothing happened. His face turned purple.

"Are you all right, Mr. Thataway?"

"Shh." His tall, lard-sculpted hairdo trembled. Pale green spittle bubbled in his mouth corners . . . and a bead of blood emerged on the back of his ghostwhite hand. He gasped for breath and the color drained from his face. "I have four million and twenty-six pores on my body. I can control all of them. I can tell them what to do." He lifted his hand. The bead of blood flowed onto his thumb. "I told that pore to bleed. The fucker bled." He licked it off.

Dr. Acton said, "Where are you going. Where have you been."

"Are those questions?"

"Questions."

"Your voice didn't rise when you put them to me. Generally one's voice rises in tone throughout the course of an interrogative statement. Yours didn't. Are you sure you asked me questions? Or were you simply thinking aloud?"

The doctor scratched his beard.

"I come from the west," said Thataway, "where I formerly lived as a westerner and a rifleman. I gave up rifles, though. And I gave up the west." Gunsmoke seeped out of Thataway's nostrils. Dr. Acton could smell the powder. "Now I've got no place to go and nothing to do. Without territory, without purpose, there can be no identity. I lack selfhood. I emit the stench of nonexistence from every orifice. I'm the ghost of somebody's dead ulcer. I'm stardust." He spoke in a grim monotone. "That's where I'm going. That's where I've been."

Deputy Baker removed his eye from the peephole of the door to the holding cell. "He's not taking this seriously," he whispered to Deputy Alias. "He's toying with us. If we don't do something, he's gonna kill all of us."

"Sometimes people get killed," said Deputy Alias.

Nodding, Dr. Acton put his briefcase on the card table. It was a burgundy eel-skinned briefcase with gold fixtures. He entered a combination, snapped open the fasteners, and removed a stack of large cards. "Rorschach!" he blurted. Then, calmly: "I'm going to show you a series of images. When you see them, tell me the first thing that comes to mind. You know the drill. We all know the drill."

Thataway smiled and sprayed his mouth.

"Here we go."

Inkblot #1: "Stupider'n me."
Inkblot #2: "Stupider'n me."
Inkblot #3: "Stupider'n me."
Inkblot #4: "Stupider'n me."
Inkblot #5: "Stupider'n me."
Inkblot #6: "Stupider'n me."

The seventh image was pornographic. Fellatio. The woman: middle-aged, fat, platinum perm, mole on overlip, too much makeup, tight garter belt, fishnet stockings, boots laced to the knees. The man: twentysomething, emaciated, hairy legs, hairy chest, feathered hair and mustache, fevered grin . . . Dr. Acton apologized and hurriedly stuffed the picture into his jacket. Then he showed Samson Thataway a black-and-white photograph of an overturned tricycle in the street.

Instantly enraged, Thataway slammed a fist into the table, chopping it in two. Dr. Acton had been leaning against the edge of the table and fell headlong into the rubble. Thataway helped him to his feet, pointed a finger in his face and said, "That was a trick."

The doctor gulped air. "I do not practice trickery, sir," he rasped. "Only truth. Only that which can be enslaved by the shackles of Reason."

When Gazes Collide

A stranger walked down the hallway of a cellblock in slow motion, the sound of clinking spurs out of synch with the heels that struck the cement floor. Periodically the action was interrupted by freeze frames that only lasted a few seconds before returning to slowtime. Credits snapped onscreen in a commanding font during the freeze frames. For instance:

SAMSON THATAWAY

The cells were empty, for the most part, although the stranger neither cared nor noticed . . . until he passed the final cell.

FELIX SOANDSO

The camera cut back and forth between the men's faces, zooming in on eyes like metal slots, on eyes like cracked eggs, slowtime slipping into superslowtime, superslowtime threatening to congeal altogether, solidifying the gravity of the exchange, but there was no stopping, and the camera went back and forth, back and forth, back and forth, until all the screen showed were the men's irises and pupils, and they were the same color, same shape, same feral glint, and the keen viewership couldn't distinguish between them . . .

Samson Thataway polished a gun with a bandana as he eased into the daylight.

Scene in Stop-Motion Animation

Pataphysical shot of the moon from outer space à la Georges Méliès. The earth sneaks up behind the moon, opens a beaklike mouth and devours it. Burps. Smiles. Lights a cigarette. ZOOM IN on the United States. ZOOM IN on the Midwest, centering on Indiana. Continue to ZOOM IN until the state completely occupies the screen. Something beats like a heart in the middle of the state. It becomes clear that it not only beats, but bleeds, and burns.

ZOOM IN on the wound . . .

Throughout the scene, the Fuming Garcias and the Dreamfielders slip back and forth between figures composed of flesh and figures composed of Plasticine clay.

Red sunglasses pulse with light . . .

They blindfolded twenty Dreamfielders, lined them up against the brick wall of the Third Financial Bank, and gave them the option of smoking cigarettes or eating double cheeseburgers. All but two selected double cheeseburgers. As they scarfed down their last supper, an arbitrary Fuming Garcia asked if anybody had a final request.

"Another double cheeseburger please!" one of them shouted. The others said quiet prayers and crossed and recrossed their chests.

The Fuming Garcias took turns firing at the Dream-fielders with a Rock Island Arsenal 1917A1 Browning machine gun. They fired long after everybody had died. Swarms of bullets tore their corpses apart, layer by layer, shredding and vaporizing fabric, skin, hairdos, tissue, internal organs, down to the naked bone, and then the bullets assailed their skeletons, a few of which were riddled to their feet, or at least to their haunches, and the skeletons did a death jig, but not for long—the bullets quickly disintegrated them, reducing them to fine powder—

The Fuming Garcias stopped firing. Their red sunglasses stopped pulsing and dimmed.

They stayed until the soot cleared.

They packed up the gun, put it in the trunk of a LeBaron, got in the car and drove away.

45

Fourth Theory of Ultraviolence

In the first chapter of *Savage Cinema: Sam Peckinpah and the Rise of Ultraviolent Movies*, Stephen Prince writes: ". . . the outré images of violence . . . a glob of (walking) gunk. . . . how palatable graphic screen gore now is. . . . contemporary movie gore . . . Sam Peckinpah is the crucial link between classical and postmodern Hollywood, the figure whose work transformed modern cinema in terms of the stylistics for rendering screen violence and in terms of the moral and psychological consequences that ensue, for filmmaker and viewer, from placing brutality at the center of a screen world. . . . his work became synonymous with graphic, slow-motion violence . . . dubious sobriquet, 'Bloody Sam' . . . the rapid and sad decline of his talents after 1974 . . . abhors conformity, is fascinated by wildness and criminality, and seeks a code of conduct to keep the terrifying void of existence from overwhelming the fragile self. . . . cruelty and sadism . . . a cathartic and ennobling function. . . . 'I get into too many problems, I drink too much, and I get into too many fights' . . . 'Everything I do comes out of anger' . . . the exploding squibs that became so dominant . . . spurting blood . . . 'gore goes too far' . . .

the new film sadism . . . The violence of that film, and of Peckinpah's work in general, fed off of the climate of violence endemic to the era and was a conscious response to it, not a mere reflection of . . . destruction . . . Peckinpah wanted his screen violence to lead viewers towards greater self-knowledge and control of their own darker appetites . . . *The Wild Bunch* . . . *Straw Dogs* . . . *Bring Me the Head of Alfredo Garcia* . . . alienation and bitterness . . . ironic sense of life. . . . and because the blood in his films had been overwhelmed by the newer and more flamboyant gore spectacles of Scorsese, Tarantino, Verhoeven and others. We now turn to an exploration of these multiple frames of perspective" (1-45).

Prince further enunciates Peckinpah's use of montage as a vehicle for representing the dynamics of ultraviolence. Film is itself a montage, i.e., a series of disjointed shots that are cut and pasted together to form an (anti)cohesive whole, i.e., film is itself a violent mode of production, one that necessitates the mangling of literal and/or metaphorical celluloid. This dynamic reifies the ultraviolence that Peckinpah shoots, edits and stylizes onscreen. Furthermore, this screen ultraviolence is almost invariably extrapolated by Peckinpah from some form of real-world ultraviolence that flaps across the wasteland of History like a galactic burning flag. And this real-world ultraviolence stems directly from the desiring-machinery and dream factory of the human psyche, which, according to some psychotheorists, philosophers and gun owners, is a repository of aggressive energy, i.e., our minds always-already imprison countless brutarians, i.e., deep down all we want to do is fuck shit up, i.e., the nature of desire is ultraviolent . . . But this is a simple, pessimistic, and commonplace view of the human condition frequently made in an attempt to justify various body horrors (e.g., wars, holocausts, murders, etc.). An innovative theory of ultraviolence must account for the softer side of mankind. We are not, as Sheb Wooley suggests in his 1958 novelty song, thoroughbred purple people eaters, after all. Ultraviolence has limits. And it requires vast stores of quiet gasoline.

46

Meatballs, Coffins, Sociosexual Ferocity & an Apocalypse of Flesh

Gil Hiskey bit into a Swedish meatball and nudged Carol Roxdale with his elbow. "Helluva thing, isn't it?"

"Ow," she said. "What the heck're you elbowing me for? I have a bruise there." She rubbed a fold of skin on her arm.

"Sorry." He glanced at her arm. There was no bruise.

Gil finished the meatball, belched obscenely, and used a toothpick to fish another one from his plate. "Can I have one of those?" asked Carol. Gil frowned. She picked up a meatball with her fingers and stuffed it into the febrile O of her mouth.

Chewing, they stared down at the coffin. The face of the corpse inside had been slathered in a layer of cheap white frosting with bright red paint slashed across the lips. Swollen eyes threatened to burst from their sockets. The corpse's mouth was open wider than humanly possible. Its tongue had curled into a diseased knot.

"I couldn't get that mouth shut," said Benedict Veit in a somber voice, appearing beside Gil. The mortician wore a black cape with a collar so tall it concealed most of his face. "I tried everything. I even put the head in a vice. Nothing worked. Then I ran out of embalming fluid. I had to improvise. It's been a long day." Gil nodded in feigned understanding. Benedict said, "Can I have one of those?"

There was only one meatball left. Sighing, Gil handed the plate to the mortician and ducked over to the buffet table. Carol regarded the two men icily, then proceeded to the next coffin.

Scores of coffins had been arranged throughout the funeral home. They didn't have enough room, so some of the coffins had to be set up in closets, storage spaces, the kitchen, the lounge of the women's toilet, and the gift shop.

Countrified slow songs of the Beach Boys poured from an unseen pipe organ while men in vulture costumes replenished the buffet table and attended to the grievers' general needs. Nobody was allowed to leave the wake until they passed a lie detector test proving that they had exerted a sufficient amount of misery.

"What does 'sufficient' mean?" asked a man who had been strapped into a polygraph machine that jabbed subjects in the arm with a pin as a vulture-man asked subjects questions and analyzed electroencephalographic activity. "That could mean anything."

"It means what we say it means," croaked the vulture-man. "Please obey the rules and answer the question."

The polygraph stabbed the subject. He screamed.

The vulture-man rearranged his beak. "Apologies. But pain is the doorway to truth."

Dejected, the subject answered the question.

"I'm afraid you're not sad enough," said the vulture-man, shaking a narrow pinhead. "Please visit the gift shop. There are smelly erasers shaped like spaceships for sale in the gift shop. The purchase of one or more said erasers may brighten your spirits to such a degree that those very spirits can then be demolished like a house of cards that rises into the troposphere."

He unstrapped the subject from the polygraph, cut him loose, and strapped down the next person in line, an elderly woman in a sequined burlap dress whose weight approached 300 lbs. The polygraph jumped the gun and began to stab her as she tentatively lowered herself onto a bench. She didn't feel it.

Across the room, another elderly woman in a sequined burlap dress said to another elderly woman in a sequined burlap dress: "Remember when the world was different? There was no violence. People didn't die. They lived and lived and then one day they started dying. Then everything went straight to heck. Remember that?"

"No," said the other woman, using a Shamwow!® to wipe sweat from her brow and face. Winded, she sat on a nearby cushion. They didn't say anything to one another for five minutes; they stared at the procession of mourners. Then the other woman said, "Goodness. All this goddamned sitting down is making me tired. I gotta get up." She failed on the first effort. And the second. And third. Her companion took her by the elbow and tried to jerk her upright. Didn't work. She jerked harder . . . and hurt her wrist. She collapsed onto the bench next to her. They rested for awhile, then grunt-struggled to stand again . . . and again . . . and again . . .

Ronald Ronman bit into a deviled egg and said, "I saw the whole dang thing go off. I was in Footland! I saw what those bastards did. I wish I hadn't seen what they did but I saw what they did."

The couple to whom he spoke had stopped listening to him and began to kiss. In the open coffin between them lay a corpse that had accidentally been put in upside-down, construction boots resting on the glossy polyester pillow.

"Then I saw some things, all right," Ronald Ronman continued. "Like when they hung those folks by their toes and slashed their Achilles tendons with them Rambo knives, one by one, right on down the line, like in a factory, like they were just doing a job. Heels were crapping blood. Crapping blood into the sewers." He stared at the egg, suddenly shocked by the neon yellow color of its stuffing. "I wonder how many movies there's been where folks get their Achilles tendons cut in two."

The couple fell to their knees. Their kisses had become more passionate, almost forced, definitely awkward, yet raw and real, as if kissing was the only thing that could assuage their virtual grief.

"Let's see. In *Pet Cemetery* that guy from 'The Munsters' gets his heel cut by that little undead boy. Gabe was his name, I think. Kevin Bacon gets snipped by the warden of Alcatraz in *Murder in the First*. Who played the warden? Uma Thurman slashes this rapist's heel in *Kill Bill: Vol. 1*. Buck. Happens to some asshole in *Hostel*, too, I think. And that's just the tip of the iceberg . . ."

Now they groped at one another, and their hands found their way into the gaps of their clothes, slipping between buttons and into open zippers, feeling, squeezing, sticking . . . They grew more conspicuous. Mourners observed them on the sly. A few followed suit, abandoning their hors d'oeuvres and resorting to explicit enactments.

"What's the big deal? What's so creepy about hacking off an Achilles tendon? I don't understand people."

As more and more mourners turned to sociosexual ferocity, Benedict Veit got nervous. If an orgy unfolded . . . somebody might sue him. Somebody always sued him. Morticians got blamed for everything. Never put more than two bodies on display at a time, he reminded himself. More than two bodies—it's too much mortality for people to bear.

"Please refrain from sexual activity," he announced, then reached out and stroked the autopen of the polygraph with an eager finger. His eyes closed, a moan escaped his lips . . .

Feathers erupted from the pear-shaped bodies of vulture-men . . .

. . . apocalypse of flesh . . . double chins hanging and swaying back and forth and pulsing like jellyfish . . . Suddenly, unexpectedly, everybody got their clothes on and stormed the gift shop . . .

In a dark corner, faraway from the buffet table, the aperture of a coffin framed the blank face of an angel. Nobody passed by her except a Dreamfielder who had made a terribly wrong turn on his way to the buffet table . . . Above her head, in large holographic letters, dangling like the trinkets of a crib's mobile, the word, the name:

HELEN

"Man Stands Deformed to See His Deformity in Any Other Creature than Himself"

Spoken by one Daniel de Bosola in John Webster's *The Duchess of Malfi*, an early seventeenth century Elizabethan drama that is perhaps history's most dynamic revenge tragedy, second only to Shakespeare's *Hamlet*, yet *Hamlet*'s longstanding success can be attributed at least in part to its media (mis)perception and (dis)ambiguation, whereas *The Duchess of Malfi* has been widely neglected and/or derided by critics, dead and alive, primarily because of Webster's transparent affinity for blood and guts. Filmmaker Sam Peckinpah met with the same resistance throughout his career, despite moderate success here and there, but in the end he died a lonely, drunk, crazy asshole and his movies went down in history as little more than hypermasculine gorefests. At best, they are remembered as *arty* hypermasculine gorefests. Likewise with Webster. The only difference between Webster and Peckinpah is a mustache, a pair of mirrored sunglasses, an exploding squib, an Amerikan accent, rampant whoring, innovative slow motion techniques, freeze frames, endless supplies of booze and cocaine . . .

48

Felix Soandso Breaks Out of the Clink

This happens: Deputy McKinney falls asleep doing dumbbell concentration curls. He sits doubled over in a rickety wooden chair, one arm limp at his side, the other arm still gripping the weight with elbow resting on inner thigh. He wears an English Bobby hardhat. He snores with locomotive authority and regularity.

This happens: Felix observes a set of keys, curiously within reach, curiously positioned on the edge of a table. He reaches through the bars of his cell and fumbles for the keys with curious fingers . . .

This happens: A furious montage of imagery passes across the delicate, ambient skin of Felix's consciousness. The onset of imagery is affirmative, affectionate: shots of Helen laughing and Helen glancing coyly over her shoulder and Helen stroking Felix's hair and Helen experiencing authentic orgasms beneath the weight of Felix's thin frame . . . Love threads into Hate. Shots of Felix and Helen fighting. Corded necks, bloodshot eyes. Then Helen vanishes. Or rather, she is superimposed by Samson Thataway, laughing, drooling, fucking, killing . . .

Spurt of blood across the skin of consciousness.

Another spurt. Another, weaker spurt.

And then: Felix Soandso robs Deputy McKinney. The only time he robbed anybody before was in the fourth grade when he stole a miniature Amerikan flag from a Wal-Mart. His mother wouldn't buy it for him. So he stuffed it in his shirt. When she found out, he had to return to Wal-Mart, give back the flag and apologize to the manager of the store. The manager looked down at him hatefully, eyes burning with the fires of Orc.

And finally: Felix Soandso polishes a gun with a bandana as he eases into the daylight.

He drops the gun on the sidewalk, breaking it . . .

Precious Blood Church

Mayor Hangmann struck a gavel against the lectern of the Precious Blood Church. The gavel had a crack in it and broke in half. He replaced it with his fist, but he struck the lectern too hard, injuring the blade of his hand. He kicked the lectern in frustration and stubbed his toe. He hopped around the pulpit on one foot, shouting curses at a giant stained glass window in the steeple. He tripped and fell onto his knee. His indignation flourished.

The congregation blinked at him.

The mayor rolled onto his back, closed his eyes and remained still.

He opened his eyes. He stood, legs wobbling. He apologized and urged the congregation to be generous vis-à-vis donations for a new gavel. It was not a church matter, per se, but gavels were nonetheless important, he assured everyone, especially in his line of work. He snapped his fingers. Makeshift deacons hurriedly passed around trays into which the congregation deposited spare change and IOUs.

"Praise the Land of the Free and so forth," said Mayor Hangmann. "Thank you for coming etc. I hereby call to order and so on. The point is: we need to do something. The strangers are out of control. We need to control them. We need to get them to follow the rules. We must convert them into ardent rule-followers."

A large man with a frizzled white beard lumbered to his feet, climbing up the shaft of his cane with quick jerks of his hands. He smacked his lips and said, "Where would we be without rules?" He sat lumberingly down again, exhausted.

The mayor made a prolonged hamster face, simulating contemplation of the old man's opinion. "That's precisely my point, sir," he agreed. "That's precisely what we are up against."

Now an old woman stood and, breathing heavily, squeezed into the aisle from the pew. Bruised cankles emerged from her shoes like muffin tops. She shambled down the aisle towards the mayor and said, "It's high time you put an end to this foolishness." She paused to mop her brow and catch her breath; standing up had caught her off guard. Then she proceeded forward again. "I says it's time to stop all this foolishness Mr. Mayor and put our faith in the Lird. It's all about the Lird. It's all about Jesus." Grunting like a *rikishi*, she lifted her arms above her head. "Ain't nothing we can do about them assholes. Hell, nobody likes the rules broke. But sometimes they get broke just the same. Lird help us. There can't be no goodness without no sin. We have to try to be good people now and hope Jesus works all this shit out for us. If he doesn't, well then that's just what he wants. And that's just what we're gonna give 'em." She heaved her arms overhead again.

The congregation burst into geriatric applause.

She nodded at the mayor for a duration that bordered on the severely peculiar and uncomfortable, then turned and went back to her seat. Ushers assisted her into the pew, pushing from behind.

Mayor Hangmann gestured for everybody to quiet down. "Thank you, Glen and Alice, for those careful words," he said. "Look here now. I love the Lird . . . Lord. I love my Jesus. But I ain't Jesus. And no war was ever settled by turning the other cheek. Make no mistake. This is a war. We are under attack. We got to do something. Now think. What are we gonna do?"

. . . The tall oak doors of the Precious Blood Church exploded.

One door flew across the church and slammed into a stratum of organ pipes. The other door toppled onto a stratum of pews like a slab of concrete, crushing the people beneath it.

Samson Thataway stood in the wrecked cavern of the entranceway. Sunrays beamed from the corona of his dark bouffant and cast in shadow the Fuming Garcias that surrounded him except for their pulsing red sunglasses.

Some Dreamfielders ran for cover. Most of them, however, were either too overweight or too elderly to move quickly; they bowed their heads and accepted their fate.

Thataway strode out of the light into the church and paused at the top of the aisle. A sultry mucous leaked from his navel onto his crotch and pant legs. He sprayed his mouth with a two gallon bottle of computer cleaner.

(ZOOM IN to EXTREME CLOSEUP on Samson Thataway's grisly speakhole . . . Like a crater infested with diseased, sucking leeches. Like an untreated gunshot *wound that has festered and decayed, oozing green pus. An inhuman speakhole, a soaking speakhole. A mad, rotten speakhole. A gash of impossibility)* . . . It spoke in a low, indistinct drawl: "Come on, you lazy bastards."

They used bazookas and grenades and Uzis to destroy the church, burying the dead in its rubble. As always, the action moved back and forth between realtime, slowtime and poignant freeze-frames.

Rape Scene

The screenwriter-filmmaker refuses to put it down in words, notwithstanding the demands of the actress-victim, so that she knows what to expect. She threatens to walk off the picture. The screenwriter-filmmaker gives in and writes the whole thing down. The actress-victim is horrified—she "can't do those things." The screenwriter-filmmaker threatens to rape her. She says she'll do the scene as long as the focus is on her eyes. She'll give the screenwriter-filmmaker what he wants, she promises, with her eyes.

She pulls it off without showing pubic hair.

51

The Nature of Rejektion

Samson Thataway was throwing knives into a corpse he had stuffed with hay. Somebody or something had taken gruesome bites out of the corpse's legs, arms and abdomen. An uneaten carrot stuck out of its mouth.

Thataway paused to empty the spigot in his navel. He resumed knife-throwing . . . and paused again after two throws. "I'm bored," he said. "I'm gonna go into that cornfield over there." He pointed. "Then I'm gonna go swimming in that lake over there." He pointed. "Then I don't know what the fuck I'm gonna do."

The Fuming Garcias traded Spanish whispers.

Samson Thataway marched two and a half blocks . . .

He surveyed the great wall of stalks. Rows and rows stretched to the horizon in a flawless geometric grid undisturbed by the slightest hill, knoll or mound of earth. This was sheer flatland, for miles and miles. In the distance, looming over the corn, colossal utility poles, pylons and power lines commanded the sky.

Thataway chose an aisle and went into the cornfield.

There was a humming noise.

He stopped. He looked over both shoulders. He grinned. He sprayed the grin with computer cleaner.

He went forward, leaving obscene imprints in the brittle soil with the soles of his cowboy boots.

The humming grew louder. Sharper. A vibration. Something was vibrating . . . Everything was vibrating.

The ears of corn had been chemically mutated into garish caricatures. They stood erect, tumescent with fertility, projecting from their respective stalks like overfull balloons.

Thataway's line of vision closed on a single ear that buzzed like an electric razor. He sprayed the ear. It produced a metallic growl.

He reached out and pinched the tip of a leaf. With a quick jerk, he shucked the fucker.

A roaring chainsaw exploded from the casing. As if anticipating its emergence, a host of nearby ears did the same, bursting forth and lunging at Thataway with revving metal teeth. He shirked the brunt of the their aggression, but by the time he escaped the cornfield, he had been severely nipped, his body a mosaic of grisly flesh wounds.

He ripped off his black clothes as he staggered towards the lake. Behind him, the corn laughed like a *derecho* . . .

Faint, he stood at the foot of the lake wearing only his boots and a pair of tattered Fruit-of-the-Loom briefs. Blood flowed freely from the lesions and gashes that covered his monochrome body, running down his chest and dripping off the sphere of a small, hard potbelly. He sprayed computer cleaner onto some of the wounds. The ecstasy of pain was cosmic, unbearable, beautiful.

He dropped the computer cleaner and strode into the lake. He smelled something funny. Stopped. Looked around. Looked up and around. Looked down.

Smoke frothed and hissed and the water bubbled at his calves. Thataway cocked his head, contemplating the gravity of the situation.

His feet and ankles were melting.

He dove out of the lake, landing on his stomach, and he bounced up and over onto his back, as if flipped like an omelet.

He arched up his head to look at his feet. His potbelly blocked the view. He rolled onto his side.

. . . timelapse of a rotting animal . . . preternatural excrescence of meat . . .

Flesh decomposed and putrefied before his eyes. In places he could see the polished bones of his lower legs. Smelled like sulfur. Felt like . . .

Samson Thataway's fingers trembled as he reached for the spray bottle . . .

52

Aide Memoire, or, The Boy without a Face

Dreams of James Colburn, Kris Kristofferson and Ernest Borgnine. They have feathered hair. Borgnine has on a wig. Dust devils play between their legs as they intermittently spit globs of tobacco juice and nitroglycerine over their shoulders. Soft explosions, plumes of dust. Nearby a boy without a face kills a Gila monster. He slices open the monster's belly and produces a ballet of blood.

53

The Weird Disaster

This is what happened: an arbitrary Fuming Garcia leaning against a brick wall was reading a book called *The Weird Disaster*. The cover featured an emerald green mushroom cloud with an archetypal pulp science fiction alien bobbing helplessly on top, as if the alien had been unexpectedly shot from the blowhole of a whale. It wore a hypertrophied brain on the outside of its skull and had on a bowtie. It was as comical as it was dead serious.

54

Felix Soandso Goes to China Wok

He wasn't paying attention and they nearly trampled him as he walked past the Dollar Store. He ducked out of the way and watched them waddle in and out. He had seen some of them before, somewhere, in the not-too-distant past. He even remembered one of their names. But that's all they were. Names. Faces. Fatbodies. Figuratively there were no round characters. Everybody was flat. The new flesh.

He dashed across the street to the China Wok restaurant and arsenal.

"Help you, sir?" said an Asian woman behind the cash register. She wore a slipshod kimono. Her long ironed hair fell all the way to the floor.

Felix looked around. He had never been inside the China Wok. He walked by it every day on the way to work and always meant to at least peek in. But he had been too tentative, too apprehensive. Too frightened.

There were long buffet tables in the middle of the place stacked with provisions. Featured foods included everything from sushi, raw vegetables, egg rolls, rice dishes and miso soups to pizza, potato skins, cheese-stuffed mushrooms, corndogs and triple hamburgers.

In the corner was a chef who made omelets and stir-fry. Close-quarter chairs and tables had been arranged on a patch of carpet to the right. A glass display case counter ran the length of the far wall. Behind the counter stood three stiff, old, mean-looking Asian men in white coats. Inside the counter, and hanging on the wall, were more martial arts weapons than Felix had ever seen outside of a kung fu film, although the China Wok specialized in standard fare like nunchaku, throwing stars and samurai swords.

"One please."

"One," said the hostess, signaling a shorter, plumper Asian woman with similar body-length hair; unlike the hostess's loose-fitting kimono, however, the waitress's fit tightly against the skin and made it difficult to walk straight. She came over and the hostess screamed at her in Chinese. The waitress flexed her jaw and eyeballed the hostess but didn't retaliate.

"This way, sir."

The waitress veered left and right and tripped over her hair four times on the way to the table. Once she fell down and had to be helped up by two busboys. By the time she seated Felix she was winded and didn't have the breath to ask him what he wanted to drink. Felix sat down, said he would have the buffet, said to bring him a Diet Pepsi, stood up and walked to the buffet. It took awhile. Even in the afternoon, the China Wok's eatery operated at full capacity. The tables were too close to one another and the people sitting in the chairs were too big. Felix had to squeeze through everybody on the way in and on the way out.

He filled a bowl with lo mein. As he squeezed back to his chair, somebody bumped him and he spilled the noodles on a table. The people sitting at the table regarded him with confused hatred, then collected the noodles with heavy fingers and wolfed them down.

Felix got another serving.

They were good. Better mixed with the taste of disposable wooden chopsticks. His Diet Pepsi was flat and warm.

He started crying.

He kept eating.

He didn't even know if he had loved Helen. He liked her. They had a strong relationship. But love? Maybe he hadn't liked her. Maybe he had simply tolerated her. Maybe he had even hated her. There were good times. There were bad times. There was lust. But he couldn't be sure about love.

Whatever the case, he saw things clearly now. Death invokes clarity. He wasn't that old. It was too soon. But he had learned the inevitable lesson. In the end, life will have its way with you. And death will have the last laugh, robbing you of the happy moments. Until there is nothing left. Nothing but despair. Nothing but a great lack and the violence you inflict in order to fill that lack. Which cannot be filled. Which is a box full of screaming holes.

He finished the lo mein and stopped crying. He got a third serving and ate it next to the buffet so that he didn't have to negotiate everybody. He ate a fourth serving. Then he paid the hostess and walked over to the arsenal.

"You want weapon?" said a worker unenthusiastically. "You want kill things? You want—?"

"Hello," interrupted Felix. "What do you have other than the usual stuff?"

"Usual stuff? What? This not usual. This special." He swung his arms in wide circles. The other two workers sniggered. He shook his head. "You go away now. Come back when get brains."

"There." Felix pointed at a weapon on the wall near the ceiling. "What is that?"

"Ah!" Suddenly excited, the workers fought to get down the weapon. The man he had been speaking to won. "This fantasy axe," he bleated, admiring it. "This limited edition Volkoth fighting axe. Buy one get one free. Also come with rubber throwing star! Good for practice, this."

Felix took the weapon. It had opposing stainless steel acid-etched blades and braided leather-wrapped handles. It was light. He could see his reflection on the surface of the blades.

"Peckinpah," announced Felix, placing the Volkoth on the counter. As he waited to be rung up, he opened the locket hanging around his neck. There was a face inside of it. Black and white. Plain features. No smile. He didn't recognize it.

55

Revenge Is a Dish that Is Best Served with Shitloads of Gore & with the Antagonist Being Forced to Eat His Own Hand before Getting His Head Hacked Off with a Pair of Fantasy Axes & with Inevitable Residual Feelings of Unsettledness & Helplessness & Fury & Atheism on the Part of the Forlorn Protagonist & in the Aftermath & before the Aftermath Perception Shifts from Cartoon Comedy to Gothic Horror to Pastoral Dystopianism

Samson Thatway sprayed his mouth with computer cleaner and eyeballed the hustler.

The hustler said, "All right now. You gotta spot me now. Gimme the seven ball at least."

Thataway said, "Ok. Take the seven. Tell you what, here's what I'll spot you. You win. No matter what you do, you win. That's my spot. Hit the ball."

Excited, the hustler lined up his shot and—

Thataway smashed the hustler's head into the pool table with a mallet. The junk of his brains flowed into a side pocket.

"You win, fucker!" exclaimed Thataway. He shouted at the dead body for awhile, then coolly signaled for a waitress. Bruised and damaged, she hurried over, holding her torn skirt in place.

"Another Long Island Iced Tea, bitch." Thataway slapped her across the face. Her head snapped back but she didn't fall over. He slapped her again. She flew across a table, knocking over pitchers and pints of beer. "Dirty bitch. I'll get it myself."

He clattered towards the bar. The Fuming Garcias had stitched him up all right, even if the scars on his body continued to shed odd tears of blood. They hadn't done so well with his ankles. The duct tape he had wrapped around them wouldn't hold forever.

Samson Thataway had no concept of eternity.

"W-what'll it be, Mr. Thataway?" said a bartender.

"I thought I told you to fuck off. Fuck off." He sprayed computer cleaner at the bartender.

The bartender staggered backwards, clutching his eyes. Thataway pointed a crossbow at him and pulled the trig—

"SAMSON THATAWAY!!!"

He flinched. The arrow missed its target, whizzed across the bar and sunk into a football on the mantle. The football deflated with a pathetic hiss.

Thataway turned and threw the crossbow aside. "Who the fuck are you?" he growled.

Felix Soandso stood in the doorway. He wore jeans and a black T-shirt. Clenched tightly in each hand was an ornate hatchet. "You killed my wife," said Felix.

Thataway cackled. "I've killed all kinds of people." He cackled louder. "What's another wife?" He cackled louder. "Get outta my world, shitforbrains."

The Fuming Garcias looked on idly, flicking lint from their Montana suits, cleaning their red sunglasses with cocktail napkins, or grooming their mustaches with cheap plastic combs. The bar's few patrons pursued daydreams with amplified vitality as they nursed cold beers in an infantile stupor.

"Math is simple," continued Felix. "You killed my wife. Now I'm gonna kill you. But first I'm gonna tell you a story. I'm a storyteller."

Thataway's festering jaw creaked open. "Stories are for fags."

Felix said, "A stranger drives a long blue car into a small Midwestern town and murders all of its registered voters. He quickly forgets about the murders, though, and tries to solve them. He fails. He diagnoses himself with a run-of-the-mill multiple personality disorder and blames the crime on one of his alter-egos. He arrests himself, processes himself, incarcerates himself. In jail, he writes a letter of apology to the mayor of the small Midwestern town promising him that voting booths can't whistle in the wind forever. Then he writes a—"

"Boring!" roared Thataway.

(WIDE SHOT of Felix Soandso from across the room. ZOOM IN to EXTREME CLOSEUP on his bug-eyed, purple-with-rage face. Camera trembles and bucks. Sharp flourish of brass instruments.

Silence. WIDE SHOT of Samson Thataway from across the room. ZOOM IN to EXTREME CLOSEUP on his snide, taunting face. Camera trembles and bucks. Flourish of brass instruments.

Repeat ZOOM on Felix Soandso. Repeat ZOOM on Samson Thataway.)

Repeat camerawork again . . . again . . .)

Felix Soandso screamed.

Samson Thataway screamed.

The Fuming Garcias began to roll cigarettes. Their sunglasses glowed and caught fire.

In slow motion, Felix Soandso charged Samson Thataway, hatchets cocked.

Samson Thataway raised his chin and sprayed his mouth one last time . . .

This is what happened at the end of Chapter 55: ". . . and enact the title of Chapter 55."

When it was over, they arrested Felix Soandso and put him back in prison.

He broke out of prison and walked towards the silos.

Fifth Theory of Ultraviolence

A man replaces a line of cocaine with a thousand miles of barbed wire and snorts it up a nostril, shredding the nostril, shredding sinuses, shredding retinas and brain tissue and puzzle pieces of skull—an endless bolt of noxious metal and eviscerated imagination shooting into space . . .

The radical infliction of pain, the graphic mutilation of the body, the hot evocation of gore are not recent formations. Recollect medieval torture apparatuses and application and the legendary art of war. Observe the interactions of monkeys in the wild. All that has changed is the medium, the vehicle. The mechanism by which we show each other our entrails.

Loud Gusts of "Ha!"

Silence . . .

Then an arbitrary Fuming Garcia began to laugh hysterically. His companions maintained stone-faces.

Acute smiles interrupted the stone faces.

Disposable chuckles replaced the acute smiles.

Loud gusts of "Ha!" conquered the disposable chuckles, and the loud gusts of "Ha!" evolved into incessant, fiery torrents of "Ha-ha-ha-ha-ha-ha-ha-ha-ha-ha-ha-ha-ha-ha!!!" Scores of infected Fuming Garcias laughed in this fashion until the one who started it all stopped and the ruckus devolved back into expressionless silence.

They got in their LeBarons and drove away.

Behind them, the neon signs of Dreamfield's eateries flickered back to life.

Autobiography of an Auteur

In *"If They Move . . . Kill 'Em!": The Life and Times of Sam Peckinpah*, David Weddle writes: "Sam glared at the producer, eyes sharp as two knobs of barbed wire, and said, 'Well, I've heard that shit before'."

Birth.

Father issues.

U.S. Marine Corps.

Fresno State College. Then the University of Southern California.

Filmmaking. Knife throwing. Brawling. Drinking, snorting. Fucking.

"I can't direct when I'm sober."

"The end of a picture is always the end of a life."

Producers often wreaked havoc during the editing process. Peckinpah always overshot footage and then carefully constructed tightly knit narratives from thousands of feet of celluloid. Producers never liked the final products. Too long. Too bloody. Too strange and erratic. They cut the films down, trimmed off the fat, as they saw it, (re)constructing leaner bodies of narration in which character and plot were transformed into Bodies without Organs. The weirdly disjointed final cuts overjoyed and repelled audiences and critics in equal measure.

More drinking, more snorting. But there was deep, earnest love. Nobody experienced love on that plateau.

Hospital. Shitty food.

Bitching about shitty food.

Death.

Peckinpah (1925-1984): Age 59

Loose flower petals and long-stemmed yellow roses drifted across the surface of the dark, quiet water . . .

At the end of time, in the anus of entropy, when the universe burned out and all the stars turned into black holes, the only thing that remained was a fistful of celluloid . . . It reached into the void and clanked against the cold grin of Obscurity. The scars on its body pulsed with history as moist squibs exploded from its flesh like fireworks. There was no closure. The action ended abruptly, without fully playing out, without being sufficiently developed, with too many needlessly superfluous adverbs . . . This is what happened.

Peckinpah.

PECKINPAH

D. HARLAN WILSON is an award-winning, critically acclaimed novelist, short story writer, editor, literary critic, historian, and Professor of English at Wright State University-Lake Campus. In addition to over ten works of fiction and nonfiction, hundreds of his stories and essays have appeared in magazines, journals and anthologies throughout the world in multiple languages. He serves as reviews editor for the academic SF journal *Extrapolation* and managing editor for Guide Dog Books, the nonfiction syndicate of Raw Dog Screaming Press. For more information, visit Wilson online at **www.dharlanwilson.com** and **www.thekyotoman.com**.

www.ingramcontent.com/pod-product-compliance
Lightning Source LLC
Chambersburg PA
CBHW050900180626
46814CB00007B/2812